Advanced Hold'em Volume 1

Advanced concepts in no limit hold'em

Ryan Sleeper

iUniverse, Inc.

New York   Bloomington

iUniverse books may be ordered through booksellers or by contacting:

iUniverse
1663 Liberty Drive
Bloomington, IN 47403
www.iuniverse.com
1-800-Authors (1-800-288-4677)

ISBN: 978-1-4401-8277-8 (sc)
ISBN: 978-1-4401-8278-5 (ebook)

Printed in the United States of America

iUniverse rev. date: 01/18/2010

Contents

ABOUT THE AUTHOR ♠

I've been playing poker since about 1995. Playing mostly home games until I was 21, then I started playing $1-$2 no limit Hold'em cash games at the local casino (and on the internet) as well as low money buy-ins in online and casino tournaments (all no limit Hold'em games), and running well in all areas. Right now, I'm playing levels I never dreamt I would be playing: $2-$4, $3-$6, and $4-$8 (and even higher) no limit Hold'em cash games as well as small (under $20), medium ($20-$215) and big money (over $215) buy-ins in live and online tournaments (STT and MTT, in all forms of poker, but mostly no limit Hold'em), and doing extremely well.

In 2007, I played poker professionally, but cut back on playing to pursue a career in writing, given the fact that I enjoy writing about poker just as much as I enjoy playing poker. So, I guess you can consider me a part time poker player and a part time author.

I've always enjoyed discussing poker with other poker players as well as watching poker on television. I would even take notes while watching poker or after a game was played in a home game, casino or on the Internet, to not only improve my game, but for research on writing books. I have also studied mathematics behind poker as well as psychology, which has given me a greater understanding on how today's player thinks, as well as how math takes a big roll is ones decisions.

I grew up and currently reside in the Metro Detroit area of Michigan, but plan to move to Vegas real soon. My dream is to one day become a WSOP world champion with many bracelets in all forms of poker. My favorite game is No Limit Hold'em, but I also enjoy other games like: Pot Limit Omaha, 7 Card Stud, Razz and most High/Low games. For years now I've dreamt of becoming a professional poker player and author (and now I am). My first book, *The Ultimate Hold'em Book*, was a huge success, so I want to bring you more books to further your poker education. Lately, I have been playing more poker as well as bigger games than before, so my success is increasing at a rate I can't even catch up to. But I can't complain though, I'm having the best time of my life, playing the best game in the world.

SPECIAL THANKS ♥

I would like to give a special thanks to everyone who has supported me in writing my second, and soon to be, third book. Never failing to mention all the online games, home games and casino games that helped me improve my game and research for all my current and upcoming books.

Thank you: Graylon J. & Jamie Prophet (Caleb and Joshua too), Mike Sleeper, James Sleeper and the rest of the Sleeper family (and Patricia Bono), Oliver Smith & the rest of the Smith family (Becky and Nolan), Jane Pordon, Shayna Bono, Dylan Lelo, Alex Lelo, Chaz, Blake, Dave, Tiffany, Marty Borucki, Amber Kurtz (with Jacob and Brianna), Bobby and Kirstin Wallace, Barry Gavel, Steve Narowitz, Steve Cureton, Sean Pavliscak, Jacqui Eleson, Michelle David, Stephanie Agius, Zina Ayoub, Taylor Bacigalupo, Tracey, The Bradley family, Melissa Lupro and many other friends and family.

This book is dedicated to everyone who has supported me in my first venture as an author, and those who have purchased my first book (as well as this one). Thank you for your trust in my poker skills, my writing ability and me. Your support has encouraged me to continue writing poker books.

INTRODUCTION ◆

In my first book, *The Ultimate Hold'em Book,* I talked about almost everything there is to know about no limit Texas Hold'em strategy. Now, in this 2 volume set, I'll talk about newer advanced concepts (to the average player) needed to be successful as well as some important concepts I've discusses before, but this time, I'll further your education about it. Certain concepts need to be discussed further to help you get a better understanding on the importance of it, while cutting out all the basic information behind it.

A lot of players may know some of these concepts and some may even be "somewhat" successful at using them, but do they truly understand the reasoning behind it to justify its proper use and full complexity of its purpose and its true and more consistent success behind it? If you answered "no", then don't worry, in *Advanced Hold'em* volume I & II, you'll learn the when's, why's and how's of different concepts needed to be successful in No Limit Hold'em games. If you answered 'yes", then I'm sure you'll find something new to improve your overall poker game. I wouldn't completely leave out any new information a more experienced player would require in need. This book is for any poker player on any level, especially the ones who consider themselves, "the average player, with average success".

"If you want to play poker successfully among the best players in the world, then this book is a must have. With money-making concepts that will help you understand how the professionals think and assure yourself to making better decisions for long-term success."- From the Author.

Live I've mentioned before in my first book, it doesn't matter how long you've been playing poker. New players and old will learn something new in my books. I love to play poker and I definitely love to teach poker. I've been successful, so why not try and make other players just as successful? (Or close to it – wouldn't want my "students" to overpower me) Of course, experience is the best way to improve your game and being successful more consistently, but knowing these important concepts will help you in your decision making when at the table. It will make the game flow easier and your chip stack increase rapidly, while instantly having an edge on today's competition.

Of course, you know by now that everyone plays differently, so some of my strategies may differ from the way you would play, but that's ok. To be honest I wouldn't want you to play the same as me. It would be too easy to read each other when we are the same table. I just want you to understand my perspective on how to be successful, so you'll have all the angles covered when playing your favorite game. That way when we are at the same table (with others of similar styles) it will be a challenge for the both of us. Learn when to mix it up and how to make the proper "unpredictable" adjustments against different opponents at different times.

In volume 1, I'll be discussing over 40 advanced concepts about playing a winning style of No Limit Hold'em, so that you can play amongst the professionals. Concepts like: don't be afraid to fold, playing rags like the nuts, does your opponent really have the nuts or the hand he is trying to represent, calling with nothing to steal the pot on the turn or river, playing as a professional in online or live games, traveling expenses, is bluffing overrated, playing too many hands, relying on luck, making new moves, playing certain hands obviously, knowing when you're beat, picking the right games, moving up into bigger games, television exposure, attacking the weaker players, re-raising when you sense weakness and so much more. These concepts are very much needed when playing No Limit Hold'em. Without these concepts your game will have the missing link it takes to be a successful professional. If you want to be like: Phil Ivey, Daniel Negreanu or some other professional you admire, then you must learn and understand these concepts as well as the reasoning behind them. Learn to use them correctly is certain spots against the right opponents.

You may see a professional make a crazy play at the table and you're thinking to yourself, "How could he make that play?" Not realizing they have their reasons behind that play. Their knowledge in advanced concepts has helped them make the correct play against that opponent, in that particular spot. Maybe it's time you make similar plays like your favorite player and watch your success rate increase. And with my help you'll know when to make them and why you're making them.

In volume 2, I'll talk about more concepts like: You know what? Let's make that a surprise. Focus more on these concepts first, then when volume 2 comes out, you should already fully understand these ones and then you'll be able to focus solely on the new ones displayed in the third book. But one thing is for sure, volume 2 will be just as important as volume 1, so don't miss out on that one.

Okay, here's a hint about volume 2: More advanced concepts and examples from the concepts from this volume 1 collection. You might find, in volume 2, many examples from volume 1 as well as new concepts never seen or heard about before. Who knows? Guess you'll have to wait and see.

It's a good thing you picked up this book, because you're showing me and the rest of the poker world you want to be successful even at the expense of a lesser-known author/player. It makes me feel I did my job correctly and you're looking for more ways to improve your game. That's why you're here today: to learn more about how to be successful in NLH cash games and tournaments by understanding advanced concepts needed to be at the level of a professional. So, now it's time to learn what you need to learn to be *that* successful.

I just hope you enjoyed my first book (if you read it). And I hope it helped you become a better player. You know by now, that the efforts in writing my first book was extremely hard, but it looks like it's paying off quite well, so I know you'll enjoy this one as well. I know the information in this book will definitely improve your game and move your status to that of a professional. Enjoy and Good Luck!!

AFRAID TO FOLD ♣

Too many players today are afraid to fold their hands; hands that include top pair all the way up to the second nuts. They feel since they have a piece of it or it's only costing them a small percentage of their stack, that they need to make the call. In their minds they feel they have the best hand and you're most likely bluffing or holding a weaker hand. They don't realize that their hand, under normal circumstances, is no good.

Most players today fail to look at every angle when playing a hand. Some might just look at position or pot odds. While others just look at their hand and focus only on that. To be successful, you must look at every angle you can before making a decision. Making sure everything adds up to the correct idea of what's possible at both ends of the table. From pre-flop to river, you must look at multiple angles available.

Some of these angles are:

1. Position (pre-flop and post flop). Will you be acting first, middle or last post flop? Your best position is playing hands where you are last to act on every round.

2. Understanding the type of players involved in the hand as well as the players waiting to act (especially the players in the blinds). Who are

1

the tight players? Who are loose? And who is the maniac or frequent bluffer?

3. The type of game it is. Tournament or Cash games? Each type of game requires its own set of strategies as well as separate variable decisions made.

4. Players and their chip stacks. You must always know what each player is holding, in chips, before making a decision. Who is about to go all in and who is sitting back, playing tight, with a large stack?

5. Who has been playing abnormal? Is anyone playing a different style than what you know of? Learn to adjust your game to the players who are playing outside their normal style.

6. Pot odds and outs (if you feel you're behind). Never make a decision based solely on pot odds. Make sure any other information you have gathered has told you, you might have the best hand or the best chance of improving.

7. Of course, playing your own hand. Once you have put your opponent on a hand, then your hand is irrelevant. Play their hand and play against their style until the hand is over. Hopefully you've made the right decision either: winning the pot or saving yourself

from going broke with a "professional-like" fold.

8. More on number 7: you must put your opponent(s) on a hand(s) every time you're involved in the pot. You should be doing this during every single hand and on every single street. Try and put your opponent(s) on a couple different possibilities they might be holding. If you do your homework (prior to that hand), then you should be able to narrow it down to, no more than 2 possible hands. Also, remembering to process the thought of what your opponent is most likely putting you on (in hand value).

9. Other factors like: implied odds reverse implied odds and percentage odds will be important in your decisions. Know the numbers and the expectancy to maximize your potential earnings.

10. Instincts!! Your instinct will be very important when making a decision. If you've been playing a long time and you have a good understanding on how the game and the players are playing, then your instincts will most likely be right.

All in all, you should never be afraid to fold any hand at any time. Go ahead and fold top pair, 2 pair and even sets if you feel you are beat. If you're a master at the game, then you should have no problem folding A-K pre-flop, a flush on the river or even the second nuts when your opponent is tight and pushing all in on the river. If he is an A-B-C player, making the obvious play, then you should have no problem folding the second nuts.

Whether it's pre-flop, on the flop, turn or river and you feel you are beat and/or are being priced out of the pot, then a fold is always the correct decision. Many times I have folded top pair and over pairs on the flop, 2 pair on the turn and a set on the river because I felt I was beat. And I was. I have no problem folding, because I always study my opponents' when I'm not involved in the hand and I see how they play every hand in different situations to assure myself I'm making the correct decision at the current and future time. Once I have a greater understanding on how they play, then I simply make the minor adjustments I need to make, to be successful, while making the correct decision almost every time.

Don't feel your top pair is always good, don't feel you'll hit your gut-shot every time and certainly don't feel that every time your hand is 2 pair or better that you have the best hand and should call all the way down to river, because their will be a lot of times that you will be beat. Know your odds, know your outs and most importantly, know your opponents. Making the right fold will save you a lot when your instincts, your player knowledge and your discipline all add up to the solution of you; being beat.

In conclusion, you may feel that I'm trying to tell you to fold every hand and play extremely tight. But that's not true. I'm only telling you to fold when you know or feel you are beat. If you feel you have the best hand, then you should definitely call or raise. You should be calling to extract more money (or you're on a draw, while sometimes raising with it) and you should be raising and re-raising to protect your hand and isolate to a minimum number of opponents – or you sense weakness.

I'm sure many times you'll raise with a draw, call with the nuts and re-raise with middle pair and a gut-shot, but that's okay, because your making that play based the information you gathered from your opponents during or even prior to that hand. Continue to make those plays as long as you feel you are making the right play against the right opponent.

Like I've mentioned before in my first book, any time you make a play, make sure you're making this play at the right time, against the right opponent in the proper situation. Stop bluffing calling stations and quit trying to bully the maniac. You won't be successful; you'll only have another story to add to your collection. And I'm sure by now your friends are tired of hearing; all your bad beat or bad play stories. They don't have sympathy for you, so keep the stories to yourself and avoid situations where a story might occur.

We all know when a tight player raises and re-raise you must give them credit for a big hand, so folding is a viable option. When a loose player raises or re-raises then his position and how he played the hand as well as whom else is involved in the hand will help you determine whether or not he is holding strength or weakness. If there are multiple tight players still involved in the hand then a loose player may only raise when he is holding strength. If the pot is short-handed or there are few tight players involved, then a loose player is capable of raising with any decent hand. If you're acting after him, then a call is not a bad idea if you're holding a strong valued hand as well. See how he plays post-flop to decide how to play against him. He will most likely make a continuation bet on every street, so a raise against that play might be the best play. You never know, he may back down and fold.

One of the biggest mistakes I see a player make when associated to being afraid to fold, is the action and the cards they play pre-flop. A player will limp in an early or middle position with a decent hand, like Q-10, K-6s or A-7 and when it comes around to a player in late position (cut-off seat, button or blinds) and he chooses to raise, the limpers will automatically make the call, stating they already have money in the pot, why not call and see what happens on the flop. The player and the position of the raiser should determine what kind of hand he is holding. Chances are he has you beat and you're stuck with weaker

hand, possibly out of position, relying solely on luck. What these players don't realize is that, yes, you are beat, so why are you calling? Very rarely will a player in those positions make a raise with a hand weaker than a hand you just limped in with. Plus, you're out of position post-flop (if the raise came from a player right of the button). Unless you hit a big hand, you're more than likely going to fold. Why not save your chips and just fold pre-flop? You know you're beat, but you're afraid to fold, right? Quit relying on luck and focus more on position, player knowledge and obvious plays where you know you are beat.

♠♦♣

Unknown Author:

"Good luck is often with the man who doesn't include it in his plans."

♠♦♣

DON'T RAISE JUST BECAUSE YOU CAN ♠

A lot of aggressive and loose players will raise just because they can. They have the monster chips stack and are capable of bullying the table. When they make this play, they don't realize that they're most likely making this play against the wrong opponent at the wrong time. This opponent is probably the tightest player at the table or making a play that obviously indicates strength. They may even make this play against calling stations and tight-aggressive players who are sitting there with the nuts. They're avoiding the "tells" and focusing more on the aggressive style they obtain and using their chips as sole means of ammunition.

When a player raises, they should be raising against the right opponent at the right spot, to protect their hand or to earn an extra bet, knowing that their opponent will call. When you start raising in odd spots against A-B-C players, then you're only throwing away your chips. First of all, you should know how all your opponents player before making daring raises and calls. If you don't know how your opponent(s) play in different situations with different hands, then you shouldn't be raising just because you can. Raise for obvious reason to start out, and then learn how to mix it up under correct conditions.

I knew a player where I played, who would always raise when he had the opportunity, and the majority of the time he would end up losing that hand. After a while, I decided to tell him that he needed to stop making these plays because he kept making them against the wrong opponents (I only told him this because we became closer as friends and he asked for my help). I told him, "If you're going to raise, you need to raise against loose players and maniacs who frequently bluff, not against tight players who are betting in early position or a bet that came from middle position where you know this person was most likely holding a holding a monster hand."

We all know that player knowledge is probably the best thing you can have at the tables. Even with a huge chip stack, you need to know when to slow things down, when the knowledge you have on your opponents are telling you... you're beat. Don't start raising every chance you can. Adjust your game to your opponents and start making better decisions. You just earned those chips, why lose them over a play where you knew you were obviously beat? Learn the players, and then start raising in the right spots. Raise when you:

1. Sense weakness

2. Are up against a frequent bluffer

3. Are out of position pre-flop and you have a good hand like: a middle pocket pair, to

isolate the players and become the aggressor post-flop.

4. Have a strong valued hand and want to protect it.

5. Want to earn an extra bet, knowing your opponent will call.

6. Want to force out the other players to take the pot down on one of the following streets.

7. You sense weakness and choose to raise to with an already large pot, knowing for a fact your opponent(s) will fold.

In some situations, calling is the better option. If gives your opponent the impression that you're weak and will continue betting on the turn and river. If you're playing against an experienced player and the board shows no concern for a draw, and you just flat call them, he'll think he is being trapped, and he might slow down on the hand, giving you a good chance of stealing the pot, whether you have the best hand or not. Of course, in most situations, you should be raising. You want to be aggressive with every hand you have, unless you feel playing it slow will be a better value.

A lot of players will raise with monster hands every time, not giving them the opportunity to gain full value for their hand, which usually results in no action. Your opponents will soon see that every time you raise you have a monster hand and will fold virtually every time. Occasionally you must call with 2 pair, sets and of course, when flopping the nuts. If you know your opponents well enough, you'll know when to flat call and when to raise. Always try to extract full value for every monster hand you hold. Mix it up. Don't always think you need to raise. Your opponents will pick that up and leave you dry.

One example of just calling, I remember, is when I flopped a flush and just called my opponents bet. I felt he just had top pair or a flush draw and wanted to extract an extra bet from him on the turn. On the turn he checked, so my read for top pair (kings) was correct, but I still wanted some value for my hand so I made a good size bet. He called and pushed all in on the river when a second king hit and I called instantly with my flush. He mucked his trip kings.

Here are some examples of raising.

IN THE RIGHT SPOT:

1. Raise against loose players

2. Raise against maniacs

3. DON'T raise against tight players who bet in early position.

4. DON'T raise against a calling station when you're bluffing.

5. Raise to protect your hand.

6. Raise to earn extra bets, when you know your opponents will call.

7. Raise, even with a mediocre hands or rags, to isolate to a single opponent (especially when out of position).

8. Re-raise to protect monster hands pre-flop or even post-flop to assure the win (most of the time).

9. Re-raise to force opponents out, when you sense weakness or ones who try to steal the pot.

10. NEVER raise just because you can!!!!

♠♦♦♣

Ralph Half:

"When ability exceeds ambition, or ambition exceeds ability, the likelihood of success is limited."

♠♦♦♣

DON'T ACT ON REVENGE ♥

There will be many times where you'll get out played or drawn out against an inferior opponent or a player who shouldn't have been in the hand in the first place. And I'm sure your first instinct would be to go after that player. That's where a lot of players make the mistake. You're just setting yourself up for a big fall. It may not seem like it, but you'll be putting yourself on "tilt". Mentally you're focused on one player trying to win your money back from them, ignoring everyone else at the table. There could be hundreds or even thousands of dollars slipping through your fingers, because you're focused on the player who just outplayed you or got lucky on the river with a weak draw.

In this situation you need to ignore the hand just like any other hand prior to that. Focus on the next one. Try to win your money back the right way: Attacking weak players, trapping with monster hands and getting full value for premium starting hands.

If you continue to ignore your surroundings and indirectly put yourself on tilt, then you just might go broke. On second thought, I can almost guarantee you, you'll go broke. I'm sure you're on tilt right now, thinking about the last person who outdrew you with rags. All I have to say it: **LET IT GO!**

In my first book, I talked about ways of controlling your emotions. If you read my first book, then you should know how to ignore the bad beats (and handle big wins correctly) and focus on the next hand. If you haven't read it, then I suggest you do so immediately. It has helped me though a lot of rough times.

Here are a few things it mentioned while catching a bad beat:

1. Listen to your favorite song (if you're wearing headphones).

2. Talk to other players about non-poker related subjects.

3. Walk away; take a break with food or a drink.

Revenge only gets you quicker to being broke, just like going on tilt. So the next time you're in that situation, ignore it and continue trying to play your best game. If you have time, and you're a successful experienced player, then you'll get your money back in no time. Of course, if luck is not on your side, then I suggest you leave the game and come back another day. You may have had a losing session today, but there's always tomorrow.

♠♦♣

Fay B. Nash:

"What a man really wants is creative challenge with sufficient skills to bring him within the reach of success so that he may have the expanding joy of achievement."

♠♦♣

ATTACK THE WEAKER PLAYERS ♦

This may sound obvious, but a lot of players still don't focus on trying to attack "only" the weaker players. They try attacking the stronger players to make them feel good. Of course, attacking the stronger will improve your game in the long run, but in most situations you need to focus on the weaker players; players, you can tell are newer to the game, because the stronger players will most likely take all your money.

Once you have a read on all the weaker players, then it's your job to attack them by making the right plays against them. Most new players play pretty obvious, so it shouldn't take too long to figure out how they play every hand in different situations. If you consider yourself an experienced player, then you'll need to bank as much information in your memory as you can, so that every time you're in a hand with a weaker player, you'll know exactly what to do to assure yourself full value for your hand and to definitely assure yourself in winning the pot. On some occasions, a fold will be your best option, if the weaker player is showing aggression or is calling big bets.

In my first book, I talked thoroughly on how a new (rookie-type) players play. They usually bet with big hands and check with weakness. They rarely bluff and their "tells" are obvious. Occasionally this type of player may make a play that confused you, but don't strain too long trying to figure it out. Your opponent, who made this play, may not realize what he/she just did. This type of play will be rarely made; so don't focus on that hand, simply fold and move on. Continue playing the next hands where you know you're reads are correct.

In most situations your table will be filled both: new and old players: Rookies, amateurs, and professionals. If you're in multiple situations where a weak player and a strong player are in a hand then simply narrow it down to this:

1. It should be easy to put the weaker player on the hand, so do that first. Then...

2. Take your time trying to put the stronger player on a hand.

3. After you realize what the weak player is holding, and you sense weakness, you need to be more aggressive, if with the more experienced player still involved. But...

4. If you feel the strong opponent has a strong hand, stronger than yours, then you need to slow things down. The weak player will probably be calling with his hand down to the river, whether it's strong or not, which decreases your chances of winning against 2 opponents.

5. If you feel the strong opponent is holding a weak hand, then play it as you would against a weak opponent: By being aggressive with your bets and raises.

6. Obviously, if both opponents are strong, then simply fold your hand and wait for a better spot.

Weaker opponents are there to win money the easy way. Strong opponents are there to improve your game in the long run. Pick your spots against either one of them and make sure you're making the right decisions against either one – or against both. In my first book, *The Ultimate Hold'em Book*, I talked about playing against rookies and professionals. Read that section if you haven't. It will definitely help you on understanding each player as well as how to play against them on a winning level.

♠♦♦♣

Lou Holtz:

"I think everyone should experience defeat at least once during their career. You learn a lot from it."

♠♦♦♣

DON'T TAKE LONG SHOTS ♣

A long shot is calling bets where your outs are limited to only a few cards, and you know the odds of hitting them are slim. Too many players, mostly new players, like to take long shots, because they don't know the true odds of hitting it. They feel and look at the situations as: "I have outs, so I must call". They fail to see things on multiple angles.

Here are some angles they overlook.

1. Putting their opponent on a hand.

2. Lacking the true odds and outs of hitting their hand on each street.

3. Ignoring pot odds and implied odds.

4. Position of every opponent involved and their actions prior to that situation.

Here are the 4 examples in more detail:

1. Most long shots are gut-shot draws, 2 outers, chasers (chasing for an over card: like an Ace) and etc. A lot of players with a gut-shot will look at the situation as that they have a straight draw and not looking at it as: they only have 4 outs (maybe less), failing to see pot odds or what their opponents hand is and

call to the river, missing their straight draw, and losing a big pot.

2. Players who are sitting there with a pocket pair, and miss the flop look at their situation as; all they need is another one of their cards to hit for a set. They don't look at it as; they only have 2 outs and the percentage of hitting a set on the flop is 12%, on the turn is about 8% and the river is 5%. Not the best odds if you ask me. Unless the price is right and you sense weakness from your opponent, a fold is your only choice.

3. Players who love to chase for an ace or any over card look at the situation as: they have over cards and if they hit one of them, they'll most likely win. They don't see it as: they have 6 outs; one of those 6 outs may be harmful if they hit it. A player could be sitting there with a pair already and if they hit there over card, which is matching your over card – will give them 2 pair. Not realizing that they just might lose their hand if they hit one of the cards they are chasing for. A lot of players will play any ace as well as any 2 big cards, which decreases the value of chasing, since the odds of an opponent sitting there with a matching card as you is a high probability.

4. Position is very important. You should know what players know about position and how

they use it against other opponents. Study the position, of each opponent, at hand and the actions the players are making based off that.

DON'T TAKE LONG SHOTS & DON'T CHASE. The only time it might be correct to chase is when you feel your opponent is weak (of course in that situation, you should be raising) and the bet is small compared to the pot, in a multi-way pot where no one is showing aggression. If you're getting great pot odds, your opponent is likely holding a weak hand or a draw and you're capable of outplaying your opponent on future streets, then chasing might be an option. You're better off playing a hand where you have more control of the pot, but in some situations chasing can pay off well when you hit it. Look at all the angles before chasing or calling with long shot draws. Make sure you outs are live, your opponents are weak and the price is right.

♠♦♣

Rosalynn Carter:

"You have to have confidence in your ability, and then be tough enough to follow through."

♠♦♣

PUTTING YOUR OPPONENT ON A HAND ♠

Putting your opponent on a hand is one of, if not, the most important skill you must have to be successful. You must put every opponent on a hand, every time, during every hand, on every round, but don't limit your guesses to just one hand. Put your opponent(s) on a couple of hands until the story comes together and you can narrow it down to 1, or maybe, 2 hands they could possibly be holding. Once you've put your opponent on a hand, then you must decide what the correct decision is to assure yourself the win, or in some cases, the correct fold. If you simply just play your own cards and not your opponent, then you'll fail to make any adjustments, where it's needed, to assure yourself you're making the correct decision. You will fail to see any strengths and weakness of your opponents and rely solely on the luck of the cards you receive.

If you're reading this book, then I'm sure by now you know what it takes to read an opponents hand. Studying how they play each hand in different situations, all while adjusting your game to theirs. So, should I really talk explain how to do it? Nope! I think the name of this book covers the level of play you're at, so let's skip to the next section.

Just kidding! We need to talk about some concepts in reading your opponents hand, because there might be some people who don't know how to read an opponents hand or don't choose to read any opponents hand. Some may not even have the agility to do such an important skill. It's a rarity, but they do exist. Nothing against them, but that's why we are here: To talk about it and learn how to be successful in reading any opponents hand. But in this section of the book I'm not going too deep into detail about it, just the basics (even though the title of this book is about advanced concepts – Basic skills are acceptable when it comes to this topic). In my first book, you'll learn more about different types of opponents and how they play. You'll learn what kind of hands they play and how they play them to the river. Today we'll talk about: draws, top pair, 2 pair, sets, the nuts and bluffing.

DRAWS:

Most players' play draws the same: check-call. The more experience players will bet their draws in late positions when everyone else has checked. On some occasions they may even raise with just a draw, when a player betting in early position is a loose player. Loose players or maniacs will bet their draws from early positions in short-handed pots. Like a more experienced player, they may raise with them as well.

TOP PAIR:

Top pair is played aggressively with a bet from any position. Sometimes a player will raise with top pair if there are draws on the board, while more experienced players may just flat call and raise on the turn or river, suspecting their opponent who made the bet is weak. New players and experienced players usually play top pair the same way, but the more experienced players will mix it up when the situation calls for it and his read on his opponents are correct.

2 PAIR:

2 pair is played similar to top pair: with aggression. The more experienced players may slow-play 2 pair by calling on the flop and waiting for the turn or river to raise. Players who are newer to the game will raise almost every time they hit 2 pair on the flop.

SETS:

Sets are played very similar as 2 pair. Refer to 2 pair to understand how most people play this hand. Most of the time a set will be played with a raise and a re-raise. Since most players won't be able to put you on a set, they will most likely get paid if played properly to their opponent at hand. Slow-playing a set is correct when your opponent is showing weakness. I think everyone is capable of slow-playing a set, but the more experienced players will do it more often.

THE NUTS:

The nuts are played in accordance to the players involved in the hand. Normally when someone has the nuts they will slow-play as long as they can. Newer players won't slow play the nuts as often as an experienced player would. An experienced player will mix it up depending on the opponents involved in the hand. Against other experience players they will mix it up. Occasionally bet and raise with the nuts and other times they will check-call to the river and then raise. Against new players they will play more straightforward. If the new player bets, then the experienced player will most likely just call the bet. If he checks, then the experienced player might check as well. Occasionally he will bet if there are other draws out there or if he feels the new player will call with any hand: weak draws, middle or bottom pair, etc.

A BLUFF:

A bluff is hard to read, so playing against a bluff will be determined on the level of knowledge you have on your opponent(s). Every player has the ability to mix it up when it comes to bluffing, so there's not much I can tell you on this subject. Trust your reads and trust your instincts. Making a bluff is easy, but calling/raising a bluff is hard. Professionals can call down a bluff more often than anyone else, so if you can want to make similar plays, I suggest you have do your homework and sit down against opponents you have an advanced read on. Information, tells, instincts, etc will all be a major factor when calling a bluff, so the more work you do on your opponent(s), the more likely you'll be able to call his bluff.

♠♦♦♣

Elbert Hubbard:

"The greatest mistake you can make in life is to be continually fearing you will make one."

♠♦♦♣

BLUFFING IS OVERRATED ♥

Even though bluffing is an important part of poker, it is considered overrated (at least to my opinion). Too many players strive on bluffing and less on reading their opponents and making the correct decisions from it. Don't get me wrong, you have to bluff from time to time to be successful in poker, but I think too many players bluff too much at the wrong times and against the wrong opponents.

One thing you have to consider is that everyone bluffs and they usually get away with it from to time. Everyone has bluffed at the pot on every street, one time or another, and has won the pot. Other times, and probably a lot of times, someone has bluffed at the pot and got caught. Reasons for this are because they read their opponent and the situation wrong. They looked at this particular spot and felt it was time to bluff, since it was the only way to win the pot. Failing to see that the opponent(s) still involved in the hand was sitting there with a callable hand. Strive on correct reads, not on bluffing. Don't be like everyone else. Be someone new and make him or her pay for trying to bluff you. Or make them think twice about thinking they have a good read on you when you're bluffing. Don't fall into unsuccessful bluffs, even at the expense of losing a large pot.

I'm not going to go into picking the right spots and the right opponents to bluff. I think I covered a lot of that in my first book as well as some information I provided earlier in this book. What I will continue to talk about is: why I think bluffing is overrated.

You win pots with the nuts, you can win pots by making the correct read on your opponent and you can win pots by bluffing. One of these winning strategies can backfire and make you lose a large portion, if not, all of your chips. Which one do you think it is? Bluffing? You can lose your entire stack by bluffing at the wrong time. I know it's necessary to bluff to win, but this play should be made rarely under - what most players consider - "normal" circumstances.

When playing poker you should rely more on reading your opponents correctly: are they weak or strong? Getting full value for your monster hands, and folding when you know you're beat. Bluffing comes last. Pick the right spots to bluff, pick the right opponents to bluff against, making sure you read their hand and their position correctly, while betting the right amount. You should know, at what price, it would cost them to fold. But whatever you do, don't make the bluff obvious. Don't always bluff on the button or last to act when everyone else has checked. That's too obvious. Your opponent may pick this up and start calling your bets. Mix it up and keep your opponents guessing. Find ways to bluff in weird situations. But all in all, bluff less and less if the situation calls for it (with a table of calling stations or experienced players who have an advanced degree in reading people). Bluffing is overrated, and you can win a lot more when your premium hands are getting full value and your reading abilities – sensing weakness – are at its top form.

♠♦♥♣

Napoleon Hill:

"There is one quality that one must possess to win, and that is definiteness of purpose, the knowledge of what one wants and a burning desire to possess it."

♠♦♥♣

TAKE RISKS ♦

In any poker game, you must take risks. You can't always rely on getting big cards and monster flops, turns and rivers. From time to time you must take a risk and rely on luck. Of course, when doing so you must do it at the right time. When the situation calls for it, you HAVE to take the risk, even if it means risking your entire bankroll in a tournament with a hand that is minimal in value compared to the read you have on your opponent(s).

A lot of new players will continue to take risks, avoiding other important factors, which usually results in numerous loses.

Experienced players will limit their risk and rely mostly on their reads. And that's the way you should be playing poker, for the most part.

Many times in poker (especially in tournaments) you'll be put in a situation where luck is your only option. You've put together the story of your opponents hands, the price of his bet is correct to call just on pot odds and your stack is getting low, while the blinds are increasing, but you know you're beat, but feel you have a good number of outs to win with. Calling is the only option, if you want any chance of winning the tournament. So you decide to make the call. Sometimes you outdraw your opponent and sometimes you don't, but in theory, you made the right choice. In most tournaments, that you play, you will be put to a decision for most or all of your chips. In those spots, you must take the risk; whether it's a bluff raise all in or a call against a player, you feel, has you beat, but you have a high number of out that would justify a correct call.

I hate putting all my money in knowing I have the worst of it. I hate calling any bet knowing I'm beat, but in some cases, you must make the call. You can't just rely on catching big cards and accurately reading your opponent by raising when you know their weak and folding when you know you're beat. Sometimes, when you know you're beat, you must call (or raise), even on the turn when the price is wrong. Luck is a factor in any poker game, so why ignore it and try to win without it? Gain full potential of luck and see if that day is your lucky day. Take chances in poker, but make sure it's the right time— make sure it's the only correct move there is. If you want to win and be successful in poker, then do the one thing most professionals hate to do: TAKE RISKS!!

♠♦♦♣

Norman Vincent Peale:

"Empty pockets never held anyone back. Only empty heads and empty hearts can do that."

♠♦♦♣

CALLING WITH NOTHING ♣

Now here is something you don't want to do too often: calling with nothing. Now, I'm not saying you should call with nothing on the river, unless you know for a fact that you have a better hand than your opponent. But from time to time you'll probably call with an inferior hand and end up winning with it. I mean, he could have been bluffing the whole way or you sensed weakness when he checked it down and now decided to bet on the river. A few times I have called with nothing on the river, and the majority of the time I was right. I've called with bottom pair, Ace high and even Jack high, but I made those calls because I knew my opponents game well enough to risk my chips with very weak hands. I sensed weakness and felt my hand was good enough.

In this section I want to focus more on calling with nothing on the flop and turn. You're probably asking yourself, "Why would someone call on the flop with nothing?" No pair, no draw, just rags. Oddly enough in some spots, calling with nothing is a daring, but necessary play. If you're heads up against an opponent on the flop and he is known to frequently bluff, bets out on the flop trying to represent a hand, and you can call trying to steal the pot on the turn, no matter what you're holding. Professionals will make this play more often than most, simply because they have an accurate read on their opponent. They know this opponent is most likely holding nothing or is capable of giving up the hand on the turn or river if they feel you're holding a better hand.

Whatever you do, don't try to play like the pros, but do make similar plays they make. Play your style. If you feel you have a good read on your opponents, then calling with nothing, to steal the pot on a later street, is a correct play. But I wouldn't make it a habit because you could be setting yourself up for a big fall.

Before making this call, look at all the angles. Look at:

1. All the players positions and how it affects their plays.

2. The type of players still involved in the hand.

3. Who is loose? Who is tight? Who is the ultimate bluffer?

4. Chips stacks are important; making sure no one is committed or forced to push all in.

5. Who has been known to bluff in this particular spot?

6. Can you risk "x" number chips to see if your read is correct?

7. Will the pot be short-handed? It's very unlikely your call would be correct if the pot is multi-way. With more than 2 players in the

pot, the chances of someone with a hand or even a draw are more likely.

Making this call (with nothing) is actually more valuable on the turn when the pot is short-handed. If your single opponent has shown weakness on the flop and decides to bet on turn, he could be bluffing where as a bet on the flop could mean a valuable hand depending on his position. For me though, I'd rather make the call on the flop because it's easier to steal the pot on the turn than it is on the river. Of course, he could be slow-playing a hand and now is trying to get value for it on the turn. If you feel he is bluffing, then you should be raising, not just calling. If you do decide to call, then you're calling because you are last to act on every round and you know for sure you're opponent is weak and will most likely check the river. If your opponent is known for slow playing on the flop to bet on the turn, then it's an obvious fold unless you have a hand yourself or a monster draw.

Here are some examples of calling with nothing and its proper value.

1. A call on the flop, with nothing, is more affective against a single opponent who is known for bluffing.

2. A call on the flop, with nothing, against multiple opponents is dangerous and will most likely force you to fold on later streets or result you in wasting a bet.

3. A call on the turn, with nothing, against a single opponent is only valuable when you know you're opponent is weak and will check on the river.

4. A call on the turn, with nothing, against multiple opponents is only valuable when you're holding the nuts or a monster draw and are receiving tremendous pot odds.

♠♦♦♣

Thomas Edison:

"Many of life's failures are men who did not realize how close they were to success when they gave up."

♠♦♦♣

RAISE WHEN YOU SENSE WEAKNESS ♠

This title alone tells you exactly what you should be doing: raising when you sense weakness. Whether it's against rookies or seasoned professionals, you must raise when you sense weakness. Of course, in some situations, you might just want to call to earn an extra bet on a later street, but most of the time you should be raising. Pre-flop, flop, turn and river, when you sense weakness from either a single opponent or multiple, you must raise. No matter you're holding, raise enough to force your opponents to fold. The only exception to this rule is when you're holding the nuts. In that case you want to raise to earn an extra bet, not force them out of the pot, so make the proper size raise will be determined by the type of players still involved in the hand. The looser the player, the bigger that raise should be.

A lot of players today may sense weakness during a hand, or may feel that they are not sure what an opponent is holding, but their instincts are kind of saying, "I think he is weak" or "I think he is bluffing", but never have the guts to actually raise. They are afraid of being called or being played back at. When the situation calls for it, even when it comes to risking a lot of your chips, you must raise when you sense weakness. If your instincts are strong and your reads are correct, then go with your feel and raise. Don't be afraid of being called or being played back at, because your opponent may in fact fold on the next street. He could have been on a weak draw or a have middle pair was hoping for more options on the turn.

If a player decides to play back at you, then simply fold and play the next hand (if your hand has no value). Your read may have been wrong that time, but you'll get it right the next time. If you feel he is just making a play at you, then you can re-raise him back for an amount of chips he can't call with. Make sure you have a huge chips stack before making a play like this.

If folding was your only option then hopefully you'll get to see his hand when the betting is completed, that way you'll gain information about how he plays that hand, which will help you against this opponent during a future hand with a similar situation.

TAKEN FROM MY FIRST BOOK – I remember a time when I limped in middle position with

K♣-8♠, because the table was playing extremely tight, and I didn't want to raise, because the players in the blinds always defend them and I felt they were borderline calling stations, and if I missed the flop and tried to bluff at it, they could call and leave me short-stacked or even broke. Two other players limped in.

Flop comes: J♦-5♣-5♠.

Everyone checks.

Turn comes a 3♥.

The player in first position bets about half the pot. I called. You might think that was an odd call, but let me explain why I just called instead of raising (when I sensed weakness). Like in the earlier section about "Calling with Nothing," that's the play I wanted to make. I knew he was weak, but I wanted an extra bet on the river, because I knew I could out play him. The other player at the table folded.

The river comes a 7♦.

The first position player decides to check. Not what I expected, but I had to bet out in case he was sitting there with a small pair and would fold to a big bet. Plus, I didn't feel my hand was good enough to check it down. I bet about half the pot and he instantly check-raises me. The second he did that, I thought he had a monster hand, but after a while of thinking I realized that he is the type of player that would make this play with nothing. So I went with my instincts and re-raised him back, with only king high, I remind you. He instantly folded and I won the pot.

In that situation, when I sensed weakness I should have raised, but after it was all said and done, I made the right play by just calling. Not too many situations require calling the right option, but in this spot it was correct. So with the exception of this hand, you should be raising (virtually) every time you sense weakness. Don't let your opponent steal the pot with a bluff or a mediocre hand when you know he is weak. Those pots are there to take, so why not take as many as you can. If your reads are correct, then you should be stealing a lot of pots yourself. Earn what you can, when you can. You worked too hard in your game to be losing pots that should be yours.

I remember one time in a live tournament where I raised (actually I check-raised) when I sensed weakness, and this particular play sticks out in my mind because I feel a lot of players are unable to make this daring move.

It was in the late stages of it and I was sitting there in the big blind with Q♥-9♦. A player in middle position limps in as well as the button and the small blind, I check. The flop is: 5♠-Q♣-K♣. We all check to the button, who makes a nice size bet, about 2/3 the pot. The small blind folds and it's up to me. The button could easily have top pair. He could also just have a draw. After a few minutes, and realizing that this player is more on loose side (aside from my ability to sense weakness) I decided to check-raise all in with my middle pair. Middle position limper folds and the button folds instantly showing: 6♥-3♥. My

instincts told me he was weak so I made the correct play by raising all in. When you sense weakness, you must act on it, and that's exactly what I did.

♠♦♦♣

Ronald E Osborn:

"Unless you try to do something beyond what you have already mastered, you will never grow."

♠♦♦♣

RE-RAISING WITH RAGS ♥

Re-raising with rags is not a play you'll normally make, but it is a play you need to make to be successful, and it must be done when your read is absolutely correct. Your game must be at a level where you're winning consistently, your reads and understanding of your opponents are dead on and you've playing your "a game" lately. This play is extremely hard to make, so make sure when you decide to re-raise with a weak hand pre-flop, flop, turn or river your read on your opponent (hopefully it's just a single opponent) is considered a "fact".

When you decide to re-raise pre-flop with rags, you've made the understanding that the original raise is a raise with weakness, because of a tell, or your instincts are telling you he's weak, or it's a raise because of their position (on the button). Your re-raise could also mean, your raising the original one, because you have a mediocre hand and would like to win the pot right then or you want to be the "more" aggressor when the flop rolls out. But in this section I won't talk too much about re-raising with a mediocre hand, only with rags.

No matter what position you're in, your re-raise is made based on information you gain from your opponent. You feel he is weak and you're trying to make a move at the pot. You're also trying to mix up your image to keep your opponents guessing on what you like to call, raise or even re-raise with. In this situation you may even want to show your cards to display that image. That play is up to you, if you feel it's the correct time to advertise.

If you decide to re-raise on the flop, turn or river, then that means you know exactly what your opponent(s) is holding and will most likely fold to your re-raise. First of all, you must understand that the person betting could have a decent hand. He could also be bluffing, who knows? Next, the person raising probably has a good hand, a hand worth calling even to a re-raise. Now, you're deciding to re-raise. Is that really the best option? I don't think it is. When you make the decision to re-raise, that means you know for a fact that the first person betting is bluffing (or just weak) and the raiser is trying to steal the pot with a weaker hand than it's justified to call with. And how do you know that? You must have been watching their game and their plays prior to this hand. You put together a story on each of them and came to the conclusion that if you re-raised, they would fold and you would win the pot. Of course, a big factor in your decision was their acts on previous streets. You sensed weakness so you felt the correct play was to re-raise. Let's hope your homework on these opponents and your read was correct, because it is not easy to win a pot with a re-raise holding nothing but ....rags.

♠♦♦♣

Winston Churchill:

"We make a living by what we get, but we make a life by what we give".

♠♦♦♣

TAKING CONTROL OF THE TABLE ♦

To be successful, you must learn how to take control of the table. You're thinking to yourself, "How do I take control of a poker table?" My answer is simple. Be the center of attention with your "poker" actions. Be aggressive, make others fear you, put yourself in situations where luck is on your side and win the most pots. Taking control of the table is not easy, but when done, everyone else will fear you, which results in you playing an easier game and your chip stack will always be growing and most importantly, your opponents will fold more often then they are used to. They will always fear that you have a stronger hand virtually every time.

To take complete control of the table, first you must be catching cards or appear to be catching cards by raising and re-raising – winning pots uncontested, showing the big hands and of course folding (and not showing) the successful bluffs, because they feel you have the nuts every time based on hands shown earlier in the game.

Second, you need to be aggressive, constantly. Raising and re-raising every time you sense weakness by your opponents. If your opponents feel you will always raise or re-raise they might step back and fold hands they don't normally fold, and they'll think twice before betting into you, but be careful, if they feel you will always raise their bets, they may just set a trap and decide to check-raise you.

Last, but not least, your image. Your image must be labeled as loose or a maniac (or the luckiest players alive because you're catching cards). Your opponents see you as a "lucky" loose cannon and will only play hands with you to the river when they have a monster hand. Of course in your defense, you'll be able to adjust your game and fold, knowing when they have a good hand. No need to raise and re-raise them in this spot, because at that point, you know they would only proceed with monster hands. If your image is labeled on the tighter side, even before you sit down, then you must be more aggressive than normal and appear to be playing like a loose or maniac player. Show them you can mix up your game and prove to them (as your displayed image shows) you're the lucky player at today's table.

At any poker table, there is always one person who is the center of attention. This person is usually loud and loose. Whatever you do, you must take the focus off him and place it on you. Loosen up your game when it calls for it and make aggressive plays (with a little bit of luck on your side), while winning more and more pots. Build your chip stack and structure your wins and plays, so that everyone around you sees it. After a while, the loud person will quiet down and the center of attention will be on you.

This may not work every time. You may be in a game where luck is not on your side or you're not playing your "A" game, but if this situation is asking for it, then it's your duty to take control of the table, by any means necessary. I mean, you already know that you must do whatever it takes to win, so why not make it a little easier on you, even if it means an early exit for just this one session (when in a cash-game). Trust me, in the end of that cash game (or tournament) your chip stack and your reputation will increase incredibly, when you've successfully taken control of your table.

Play with those same players again and see what happens: It will be like you never left the table in the fist place; continuing to be in control of the table and taking down pots more often. Only this time all that previous work won't be necessary. Your image is already engraved inside their heads, so all you have to do now, is continue your high level of luck and win those much-needed pots.

♠♦♥♣

Joel A. Barker:

"Vision without action is merely a dream. Action without vision just passes the time. Vision with action can change the world."

♠♦♥♣

RELY ON LUCK ♣

This is a strategy most professionals will not display. Relying on luck is not in their repertoire of poker (definitely not in mine), but in some situations you must rely on luck. If the situation calls for it, you must rely solely on luck. This section is similar to *"Taking Risks"*, but this deserves to be in its own separate area.

If you are at the table short stacked: you must rely on luck and push all in hoping you'll win the pot pre-flop or by having the best hand when the river falls. If you are getting tremendous pot odds and you know you're behind, at the same time it's not costing you too much to call, then you must rely on luck. If you're making a move to increase your chip stack in a tournament, because you'll need it to make it to the final table, then you must rely on luck. Occasionally you will make an exit, but when you don't, then it's all about the final table and that first place prize.

These are just some of the reasons why you should rely on luck, and dissect into greater detail about these 3 particular ones.

1. *Short-stacked:*

If you are in a tournament and the blinds are eating up at your chip stack, then you must find a playable hand and push all in. If someone calls you, then you will most likely be behind and rely on luck to win the hand. As of this point, you know what a playable hand is, so I won't mention them.

You don't want to be blinded out, so you decide to make a move with a decent hand to either force everyone to fold or get a caller and hope for the best. If you're fortunate enough to catch a strong starting hand, then luck may not be your factor, but it is still something you need on your side. Your opponent could outdraw you and now you're out of the tournament.

2. *Tremendous pot odds:*

On any street (mostly flop and turn), if you're getting great pots odds, but you know you're behind, sometimes you have to call in hopes of catching a much-needed card. You can't always fold in that spot and give the pot to your opponent. From time to time you must make a call to either outdraw your opponent or outplay them on the next street.

If the pot is offering more than 5 to 1 on your money, then it should be an easy call to make with almost any draw (flush draw, open-ended straight draw and maybe even a gut-shot straight draw). Sometimes just having a pair and a backdoor draw is worth calling with, when the pots odds are that huge. Of course, you shouldn't call every time the pot is offering you a huge return, but at times, when you feel you can outdraw or outplay your opponent, then it would be correct to make the call based solely on pot odds to see how lucky you can get.

3.   *Increasing your tournament chip stack:*
     This move is made mostly during the middle stages of a tournament. When the blinds are getting bigger, but your chip stack isn't increasing enough to withstand the blinds, then you must rely on luck to even have a chance of making it to the final table and evidently the 1st place prize. You must put yourself in a situation where you're risking a lot or all of your chips in a spot where you need luck to win. Push all in with a monster draw on the flop, hoping you'll get a call and outdraw him. Or maybe you feel like pushing all with just over cards on the flop against an opponent with top pair, hoping you'll hit one of your cards for the win.

     I've been in many tournaments where I felt I could do well, if I didn't rely on luck and just win pots with big hands and great calls (based on my reads). Not the best decision after I analyzed what I did. I realized that I must rely on luck when the situation called for it. I must take chances. I'm not saying I haven't won a tournament before "not" relying on luck, because I have. But I'm better off putting myself in situations where luck is a factor and where luck is the only reason why I made the move. It's a good way to have an even bigger chip stack entering the bubble when you're not catching cards.

You can win tournaments without relying on luck, but you'll win a lot more if you do. And in those situations, make sure you're making the "lucky" move at the right time of the tournament; when it's most important in comparison with the blinds, your chips and most importantly against the right opponent when you read them and the situation correctly.

In some situations you must call a bet knowing you're beat, simply to rely on luck, in hopes of catching a much-needed card on the next street. If you fold too often, you won't get too much action when you finally do pick up hand. You'll be so happy to finally have a made hand that you might play it wrong for minimum value. Knowing your opponent and the odds of improving as well as the amount already in the pot, will determine when its best to call a bet knowing you're beat and putting yourself in a situation where you must rely on luck.

♠♦♦♣

Brian Tracy:

"Develop the winning edge; small differences in your performance can lead to large differences in your results."

♠♦♦♣

MAKING NEW MOVES ♠

In any poker game, you must try new moves to not only to keep your opponent's guessing, but also to improve your game. If you keep making the same moves, the more experienced players will eventually catch on to it and adjust their game to make easier decisions against you. They will know how you play certain hands on certain streets in different situations. So, in order to assure yourself a successful sessions or a win in a tournament, you must make new moves. Experience new plays against different types of opponents until you get a feel on what "new" moves are proper and the level of comfort you're at making these new moves.

To make these new moves you must decide when is the best time to do it, as well as whom to do it against. If you know your opponents game well enough you should know when to make these new moves. Against a tight player you know when to slow play a monster hand against them. Against a loose player you should know when to bet out with a strong hand or check-call to the river. Occasionally you'll need to mix it up to be unpredictable, so you're opponents continue to guess whether or not you have the winning hand or not. But does this define making a new move? Yes, it does, but it's only some of what I'm going to talk about here.

In my first book, under *Evaluating Yourself*, I explained how this one player wanted to open his game up more. So I told him to make new moves. Make moves you don't normally make against different opponents. For example:

1. If you're known to check with draws in early position, then sometimes you must bet with your draws in early positions. *This is most profitable in a short-handed pot.*

2. If you're known to always slow-play the nuts, then on occasion you must bet out or raise with the nuts. *This play works best when you know you're opponent is a calling station or has a big hand as well.*

3. If players feel you only raise with big hands, then from time to time you must raise with weaker hands: middle pair, draws, bluffs etc. *This play will only work when you know your opponent is weak.*

Of course, to make these plays you must make them against the right opponents in the right spots. Your read on your opponents should help you out on when to make these particular plays. If you feel they have a good read on you, then making these plays must be done immediately. Show the hands that will make them second guess themselves on the style you play.

If you don't open up your game and make new moves, you'll opponents will continue to outplay you and you'll start losing more sessions and tournaments then you're used to. The stronger your opponents get, the weaker your game will get. Mix it up, make new moves and continue to keep your opponents guessing, if you want to be successful. Don't be afraid of going broke or making an early exit in a tournament. Professionals today continue to improve their game and don't settle on playing one style. They play to their opponents and always try to find ways to be successful in unfamiliar circumstances. They adjust their game, take chances on luck and most importantly, they are always making: NEW MOVES.

♠♦♦♣

Charles Du Bos:

The important thing is this: to be able at any moment to sacrifice what we are for what we could become.

♠♦♦♣

PICKING THE RIGHT GAMES ♦

Picking the right game is extremely important when being successful in No Limit Hold'em, especially in cash games. Choosing a game that is outside your limits could cost you your entire bankroll. Picking a game that is inside your limits and possibly to easy to play in, could also cost you entire bankroll, but when you choose right game, your bankroll is more protected.

Reasons for these are, when you play a game that you're not used to or a limit you haven't played before (outside your limits when moving up), you're entering a style of unfamiliar territory. You may be successful at the level right below it, but when you move up, it's a whole new ball game; new players, bigger bankrolls, higher swings and of course, smarter players. Adjusting to this level may take time, so make sure you're picking the right game at the right time when making this move.

When you play a level lower than you, you can also lose your bankroll because you're used to it and it may appear boring to you, so you make crazy plays and abnormal calls. In return, your bankroll could be slipping away right in front of you. So, in order to be successful, you need to pick the right game that not only keeps you on your "a-game," but also a level where you can be successful at. Pick a table that supports your bankroll as well as your style and level of comfort – never forgetting a level that keeps you focused.

HOW DO YOU KNOW, WHAT IS THE RIGHT TABLE FOR ME? Assuming you're a cash game player/specialist and not a tournament specialist. We will get to the tournament part next.

1. First start with your bankroll. Do you have at least 100 times the big blind?

    a. If so, then play at the table, if and only if, you have extensive experience at that level.
    b. If not, then play a level or two just below that one, until your bankroll and experience increases.
2. How much experience do you have playing at the level you want to play at?

    a. If it's less than a year, then I would advise you to either play at the level cautiously or play one level below it. To be truly successful, you want a few years of success and experience at one level before moving up.
    b. If it's more than a year, then I would say, "go ahead," just make sure you're bankroll can afford it. Let's hope your previous experience has been good to you.
    c. If you have no experience at this particular level, then maybe you should play a lower level until you bankroll increases as well

as your understanding on how the new level is played. A process like this could take months or even years.

LAST, BUT NOT LEAST...

3. How successful have you been in poker cash games?

    a. Breaking even? Not too sure you want to pick a new game or a level that is higher than what you're used to. In fact, you should probably move down a level or two until your experience and bankroll increase drastically.
    b. Winning a lot? I would continue playing at the level you're winning at. Why risk is at a new (higher) level. You obviously picked the right game for yourself, so stick with it.
    c. Losing every time? You should definitely move to a small level until your experience, bankroll and understanding of the game improves.

In any of the negative outcomes, you should try playing tournaments. It seems like cash games are not your style, so try an alternative and see how your success rates.

Any time you choose to play a cash game (for real money) you have to make sure you're picking the right game for your style, level of comfort, previous experience and bankroll. Playing a game outside any of them can result in losing it all. Players play best when they are comfort at that certain level – when they're having fun, since having fun does equal winning. Their bankroll can handle the swings, their experience is of advanced understandings and they can adjust to all the players who play at level. They have been there before and know how the pots and the players play out. If they played a level they are not used to, they would lose money, just like any other player out there today. Professional or not, anyone can go broke when they don't pick the right game.

AS FOR TOURNAMENTS...

It's all about your bankroll. If you can afford the tournament and you have time to play it to the end, then play it. I don't care if there are 10 people or 10,000 people, if your bankroll can afford it and have time it takes to play it, then by all means, play the tournament and let's hope it plays off.

If you're bankroll can't afford it or you don't have time to play it to the end, then you should play a smaller tournament until both equations improve equally. Sit N Go's are great for players with small bankrolls and not a lot time to play (when playing online). When playing live poker though, you should be able to have all the free time you can afford. Take your bankroll to a level you can comfortably play at and do whatever you have to do to take home the prize.

Of course, experience is important too, when playing the right tournament, but all in all, any experience in a tournament will help you in other tournaments. If you're a tournament player, then you should know how the structure of a tournament works and should have no problem adjusting to it and all the players. And, if you decide to start playing cash games, then slowly move into cash games. My advice is to play small, low buy-in, low blind cash games until you get a good feel how cash games differ from tournaments.

Here are some accurate buy-ins and bankroll requirements needed to be successful when choosing the right game:

CASH GAMES – No Limit Hold'em

Table Stakes/Blinds:	Amount Brought to the Table:
.01/0.02	Buy in: $2 - $6
.10/0.20	Buy in: $20 - $60
.25/0.50	Buy in: $50 - $150
.50/$1	Buy in: $100- $300
$1/$2	Buy in: $200 - $600
$2/$4	Buy in: $400 - $1200
$3/$6	Buy in: $600 - $1800
$4/$8	Buy in: $800 - $2400
$5/$10	Buy in: $1000 - $3000
$6/$12	Buy in: $1200 - $3600
$8/$16	Buy in: $1600 - $4800

$10/$20	Buy in: $2000 - $6000
$12/$24	Buy in: $2500 - $7500
$15/$30	Buy in: $3000 - $9000
$20/$40	Buy in: $4000 - $12,000
$25/$50	Buy in: $5000 -$15,000
$50/$100	Buy in: $10,000- $30,000
$100/$200	Buy in: $25,000 - $45,000
$150/$300	Buy in: $35,000 - $65,000
$200/$400	Buy in: $45,000 - $90,000
$300/$600	Buy in: $60,000 – $150,000

The first amount (in the buy in) is usually the max amount you can bring to the table, unless otherwise stated at your local casino or other game where legal cash games are being held. It's also a comfortable amount to bring without being pressured to push your stack or make constant re-buys if you lose a large pot.

The second amount is what you should bring to the table if the casino or table game you're playing will allow it. If that amount is not allowed, then this amount is what you'll need (most likely more) before playing that particular level. You always want to have at least double the max buy-in before playing that level. It gives you a comfortable state of mind knowing if you are losing, you'll be able to re-buy or move to another table with the same amount that was brought to the previous table, which stables you mentally.

A lot of players don't do well in poker because their bankroll is too small (especially in cash games). If you know you have a large amount available, your mind will be at ease and you're decisions will be made more accurately. You will unconsciously know that if you get unlucky or make a bad play, you'll have funds waiting for you near by. Of course, when you choose to re-buy, you must know that the table you're currently playing at is capable of being beaten. If you can't beat the table or the cards/luck is not going your way, then you need to find a new table or take a break from poker overall. Even though you have large bankroll, you don't want to risk it all in games you can't win.

One more thing about cash games is how people perceive and keep track of wins and loses, stating how much they made per hour. Even though this is a simple way of doing it, it's not the best way to analyze your financial states when playing as a professional. The best way to do the math in the perspective of keeping track of how successful you are, is calculating an overall number per week, per month or by per year.

When players keep track of daily records they focus on the small wins and loses that accumulate or diminish after each play. True, they may keep records on their +/- of their poker earnings at certain places and at certain games, which is very important, but overall they mentally only see the minor swings from a stand point gathered from a daily basis. By focusing on the big picture and how well they did over a period of time, they'll be able to accrue a more accurate number. Wins and loses happen all the time; luck being a major part of it, so by setting your goals and keeping your numbers over a more lengthy amount of time, you'll see the numbers even out over your poker career in ratio to the more accurate percentages the average player gets lucky or unlucky.

Here is the bankroll requirement for playing tournaments professionally:

TOURNAMENTS – No Limit Hold'em

Bankroll requirements for playing tournaments really only comes down to being able to afford it; by taking a small portion of your poker bankroll and entering the competition. Obviously, if the buy-in is too high compared to your set number of spending money for playing tournaments, then it's not a good idea to play in that particular game. A good example of the proper amount is to multiply the average buy-in by the number of tournaments you plan to play that week. If you can enter every game you plan to play in and still have a least 1/3 left of the amount it would cost to play that week, then by all means, play in every game you already had planned to play in. If it's less than 1/3, then you might want to limit the number of tournaments you enter that week (or month if that's the type of records you prefer to keep). But unless you cash in one of those tournaments, or maybe even win one of them, then you'll need to adjust your spending to the upcoming tournaments following that week, that way you're always ahead of the flow and if you run bad, you'll still have a comfortable bankroll to fall back on. If you choose to play more tournaments after you cash or win, you might end up losing it before the start of your next series of tournaments. It's always better to have a little extra, than being a little short.

♠♦♦♣

Ryan Sleeper:

"Poker is 100% luck and 100% skill. Lack of either one will result in a lost."

♠♦♦♣

LIVE GAME PROFESSIONAL ♥

Being a professional poker player is one of the hardest jobs there is. It may be fun playing poker, but earning a living from it is not easy, and on most occasions, not really that much fun, when you're stuck in a losing session, where these sessions could last months, if not, longer. Most of the time, you'll have to grind it out until you hit your big break: winning a major tournament or winning a huge session in a cash game. Other times your bankroll will fluctuate in small increments, while, from time to time taking big hits to it. You can avoid these big hits and constantly losing sessions when you accurately pick the right games/stakes as well as knowing when to leave when you sense the game not going your way.

Everyone knows you can't always win in poker. Sometimes you'll lose a little and sometimes you'll lose it all. On the rare occasion, you will win a lot, but mostly you'll win small amounts that slowly add up; just enough to keep you going. If you've been playing your best, then your wins will follow along, just make sure you know when to slow down or stop when the rush is over.

Also, learn not to hit and run when you're winning. Continue to play until you are forced out. Too many players win a big pot in a cash game and instantly leave, not realizing that other players may do that to you and if by chance you have a big losing session, you won't have enough to recover since you left the table (in an earlier game) with only a small increase in your bankroll.

When you're game is off or the cards are not running your way – or the players are out-playing you, then you need to discipline yourself and learn how to completely stop and take a break for a while. Take anywhere from a couple days to a week off (sometimes longer). Wait until you feel comfortable enough to return to poker. Get your rest, fuel your energy and make sure you're in great health (physically and mentally) before you continue. During the time you're away from poker, make sure the game is completely out of your mind. Don't read poker books or watch poker on television. Block out anything that is related to poker until your recovery is complete.

Playing poker for a living as a "live" player requires a lot more than just having the skills on the table. You must also have the skills off the table. In my first book, I talked about picking the right game that not only fit your style but your bankroll as well. Don't play a game you are unfamiliar with or a game that is too risky and too high of a level to play at. Play where you can win. Over time you'll slowly move up into bigger games and bigger limits. Your skill level and table stakes should be the factor on which game you play during the duration of becoming a true professional.

You also have to look at the traveling factor and money management, which I will talk more about later in this book. Being a professional poker player you must travel a lot. Picking the right game could mean traveling to a different state or country. Make sure you have enough "side" money to travel with. Food and other personal items are also important to factor when collecting and organizing your bankroll.

All in all, don't rush into being a professional poker player. Take things slow until you get the hang of it. Make sure your bankroll and all other personal assets are well taken care of before venturing as a professional "live" poker player. In the beginning of your career, start out as a recreational poker player. And as time (months or even years) passes by, you'll learn how to handle your money properly, pick the right games that fit your style and bankroll and adjust to the traveling and bankroll fluctuation stress and its relations, that it takes to become a professional "live" poker player.

♠♦♦♣

Nido Qubein:

"When a goal matters enough to a person, that person will find a way to accomplish what at first seemed impossible."

♠♦♦♣

ONLINE GAME PROFESSIONAL ♦

A professional poker player that solely plays online sounds like the ideal job, but it's extremely hard. Unlike, a live game professional, you don't have to deal with travel expenses, but you do have to deal with more bad beats and losing sessions, because you'll play way more hands online then you would in a live game. Also, there are more "new" players or rookie level players that play online, even playing for real money at high stakes and they are known for making outlandish plays and outdraws. In the end you should beat these players, but quite often when you play against these players and catch a bad beat, you're more likely not to see these players again, unless the software you play at has a buddy list which allows you follow them. Of course, you shouldn't follow these players too much directly, because in a sense you will be playing under revenge, which I talked about earlier in this book – not to do.

Online professionals have looked past the trust of their money not present in front of them, not being able to receive their money right away and all the distractions around your house, while "working". Most software's that condone real money (poker) games can be trusted. Sites that are not trusted are online casinos. Don't waste your money with those sites. Make sure, if you do decide to play online poker for real money that it's at a site you trust and with an amount you can afford; sites you see on television with other professionals on it as well as sites you're friends and family have played at and have experience with.

Trusted sites like:

1. Ultimatebet.com

2. Partypoker.com

3. Fulltiltpoker.com

4. Pokerstars.com

5. Absolutepoker.com

Etc…

To be a professional online poker player you must have the right skills on and off the table (just like a professional live poker player). The obvious are picking the right games and stakes, making sure when you play there are no distractions and knowing when to leave and when to stay at the table. If you're winning, then you must continue playing until you are forced out, like any positive game you have control of. If you are losing, then you must leave and either find a new table or end your session for the day. And, since you can't get your money right away, you'll need to adjust your daily spending. Adapt to what you buy and when you buy it to the weekly or monthly "paydays" you receive from Internet poker.

I don't feel I need to explain the skills it takes to be successful at poker (while on the felt), just the skills it takes to learn how to keep your money and earn more playing online poker. Any time you play poker online, it should be just for fun: either with play chips or low stakes that don't affect your bankroll or your daily spending. But if you do decide to play online for higher stakes or you're at a level that you would consider yourself a professional "online" poker player, then you must know the pros and cons of it. I figure at this point you know what tables to play at, what stakes to play at, when to leave and stay and how to handle your money, separating your poker expenses and your personal expenses, so it all just comes down to doing it the correct way.

In my first book, I talked about the pros and cons of online poker – refer to that book on more on this subject. Today I'll just explain a few of them.

PROS OF ONLINE POKER:

1. Less traveling

2. Playing in the comfort of your own home.

3. Fewer expenses.

CONS OF ONLINE POKER:

1. Can't get your money right away.

2. Lack of social interactions.

3. More hands, which results in more possible bad beats.

Online poker should be a source of practice and time consuming poker until you're able to play live poker again. Live poker is the best experience there is, so spend less time playing online and more time playing in live games, it's more fun.

Online poker is also great for satellites and extremely low stakes, trying to earn a seat into a main event at a cheap cost and trying to build some extra spending money for the trip to the WSOP. But if you do find yourself successful at online poker, then play with caution. Treat it like a real job and always play your best. Handle your money properly, pick accurate games, do your homework on all the players, evaluate your game progression, invest in a poker tracker (a program which accurately provides you with statistic on all your opponents you recently played with) and ultimately ...HAVE FUN!

REFER TO THE SECTION - *PICKING THE RIGHT GAMES* - FOR ACCURATE BUY-INS AND BANKROLL REQUIREMENTS FOR PLAYING CASH GAMES AND TOURNAMENTS.

♠♦♦♣

Oliver Wendell Holmes:

"The young man knows the rules, but the old man knows the exceptions."

♠♦♦♣

ACT ON READS ♣

Strangely enough, a lot of players do not act on their reads. They will put themselves in a situation where they have a read on their opponent, but fail to act on them. They will sense weakness, but fail to pull the trigger to raise or re-raise. Or they will sense strength and fail to fold.

Of course, folding is a lot harder to do when you feel you may have the best hand. If you read the first section about players who are afraid to fold, then you should have no problem mucking your cards when you know you're beat. If you don't know you're beat and you sense you may have the best hand, then other concepts come into play (usually determined by re-evaluating your opponent's story and how he played the hand). But, all in all, if you read your opponent to having a weaker hand than you, then you must act on your read and call or raise.

I have seen a lot of player sense they are beat and will simply call just because there is too much in the pot or they want to see your cards and feel they may have the best hand, no matter if their reads are telling they are beat or not. You can play the hand perfectly to direct to your opponent to having them beat, but they will call you anyways, because they feel they may have a shot at winning the pot. You could have played your hand perfectly for a straight or flush and they want to call you with top pair or

2 pair. They are afraid of folding a big hand even though their reads tell them: they are beat.

To be successful, you must have accurate reads on your opponents – that's a given. But to get to that level, you must do your homework and study your opponents every move and every play. Once you have a high level of reads on different kinds of players, then your reads should be almost flawless. Then, when you're in situations where your reads are important (which should be in almost every situation), then when you act on your reads, you should be correct virtually every time. Now, everyone knows that your reads can not be correct every single time, but over a course of your career, you reads will get stronger and stronger, that's if you want to be successful; resulting in more correct ones than wrong ones.

So, any time you play poker and you feel you have an advanced understanding on the game and the players, then you must act on all your reads no matter what. Your reads – also known as your instincts – will lead you to victory, no matter what the situation is. There have been many times where my reads (instincts) were correct, and many of those reads were in situations where the only information I had on them and the only play I would make against them were decided by my read. Without my reads being as strong as they are, I wouldn't have had the success I have today. I do my homework on and off the table to assure myself success. I study all my opponents as detailed as I can, and with that, has resulted in multiple wins over my career.

In the end, don't be afraid to fold, call or raise when your reads tell you to. If you feel your reads are strong, then act on all your reads no matter what. You'll be surprised how many times your read is correct. Yes, from time to time your read will be wrong, but with that only comes more information on your opponent as well as instincts on the verge of getting stronger. It may have been the wrong read this time, but the next time you're in that situation again, you'll most likely be right. Keep doing your homework (even on opponents you already know about and of their game) and keep acting on your reads. Never be afraid to make a daring playing in situations you're not sure of. Your reads will lead you to victory, so the next it tells you to do something, DO IT.

♠♦♦♣

Oscar Wilde:

"Experience is one thing you can't get for nothing."

♠♦♦♣

LISTEN TO YOUR INSTINCTS ♠

This section is similar to the previous section, but requires its own area of expertise. Reads are reads; being able to read an opponent and the value of his hand based of information you have gathered on that particular opponent, where as instincts are the ability to make the right plays on what you're gut instinct is telling you to do.

Oddly enough, a lot of players do not listen to their instincts. They will think to themselves that they have the worst of it and still call, while other think they probably have the best hand, but fold.

Any time you play poker and you're at a level above the average, you must listen to your instincts in every situation. Sometimes you'll be wrong, but most of the time you'll be right. When your instincts are wrong, that only means you have more work to do on that particular opponent. Keeping doing your homework on that player as well as other players who play like him/her and in time your plays against them will be more often right.

Many plays require your instincts to tell you whether or not you have the best hand, while ignoring and failing to recognize pot odds, physical tells and chip stacks. I've been in many situations where I even surprised myself when I'm instincts tell me to do something and I do it – and I was right. Even in weird situations (whether I'm in the hand or not) where my instincts were telling something and when the hand was over, I was correct. By watching my opponents play at all times, I see how they play certain hands in different situations, so even when I'm not involved in a hand with them I still try to figure out what they are possibly holding.

I remember one time I took third place in a tournament and I was watching the final two players play. The player on the button stuttered for a second and then limped in. The big blind checked. I thought to myself, "I think the button (his name was actually Bobby) was holding a monster hand (aces or kings)." There was action on every round, but Bobby wasn't raising or anything until the river. After the hand was the over (in which Bobby won the hand), he flipped over his cards and he showed pocket aces. Of course, I blurted out, "I knew you had a big hand like, maybe aces or kings." And I knew that because my instincts were telling me that.

Situations like that will come up all the time. If you play long enough and you do your homework in pursuit of being a successful poker player, then your instincts will get stronger and stronger and you'll be able to make daring plays and start calling the exact two cards your opponent is holding. And of course, we all know how to get stronger instincts don't we? That's right, we study our opponents every move with every hand in different situations, whether we are in the hand or not. Just by simply observing your opponents, your instincts will get stronger. Over time, your skills and your bankroll will increase so much, that one day you'll be playing on television with the top pros you see every day in WSOP or in weekly a high stakes poker cash game, where the spotlight is on you.

And, let's not forget the reaction you'll get when you name the exact two cards your opponents are holding. Skills like that will make your opponents fear you and most likely, alter their game a little, where you have a bigger advantage against them. I wouldn't be surprised if they started playing differently and folding more hands then they are used to. Sounds like taking control of the table, doesn't it? Something I talked about earlier in this book.

♠♦♦♣

George Edward Woodberry:

"Defeat is not the worst of failures. Not to have tried is the true failure."

♠♦♦♣

SMALL POTS VS. LARGE POTS ♥

The size of the pot will always vary when playing poker. Sometimes the pot will be large, other times the pot with be extremely small. But is one more important than the other? Of course, the larger the pot the better, but it also means you're risking more to win it. The small pot has an equal level on importance, in certain situations, where you need those pots: in bigger cash game or in a tournament and the blinds are going up quick. Small pots also are perceived as a laid back, low risk spot where we can win the pot without a contest, since most players focus more on the larger pots.

The large pots are obviously the pots we want simply because the more the risk, the more the reward. But a lot of players avoid large pots, unless they have a monster hand or the nuts. Few players will risk it all for a large pot with a mediocre hand or a bluff. If you want to be successful, you need to risk your bankroll in different spots, no matter what game/stakes you're playing. True, sometime you'll go broke, but from time to time, you will win that large pot. If you only play to win those small pots and only risk it all on large with the nuts, then your opponents will pick up on that an avoid situations where you could possibly win that larger pot, knowing you most likely have a strong hand.

Whether it's a large pot or a small, you must do whatever it takes to win it. Now, I know you can't win them all, but you must win as many as you can, when you know you can win them. Sometimes you have to fold in those spots, but let's hope you've learned how to avoid situations like that. Let's hope you're already at the level where you know when to avoid most, or all, of your bankroll in a spot you'll most likely have to fold, or against an opponent who calls almost anything.

The small pots are just as important as the large pots. Whether you're playing in a cash game or a tournament, the small pots make a difference. In a cash game, every pot counts, simply because you are using chips with real value and you want to make as much money as you can, when you can. In a tournament, the blinds are always increasing and you must take down your fair share of small pots to compensate for the next level in blinds. A few small pots early on can help you out with blinds later in the game. Learn to steal blinds with rags, even if your only success *was* just winning blinds. Sometimes with rags, while in temps of stealing the blinds, I'll want to see a flop, because if I hit the flop strong enough (as well as my opponent) I'll most likely get paid for a hand he would probably never put me on.

Majority of the time, I'm not worried about the small pots. I'll let my opponent take them with little or no risk when I know I'm beat. I focus more on the large pots. I will do whatever it takes to win that large pot. I don't care if I'm in a cash game or tournament, when the pot is large and I'm still in the hand, I will adjust my game completely to my opponents so that I assure myself that pot. It's doesn't always work, but I know I've taken my fair share of large pots.

Now, I don't always avoid the small pots, but I do worry less about them than the large pots. Maybe I should focus more on them than I usually do. Too late, I've already doing that. Lately I've seen more and more importance of these small pots in different games, especially in a cash game. So do what I'm doing now: Focusing equally on all small and large pots. Trust me; your bankroll will thank you.

♠♦♦♣

Michael Jordan:

"I've failed over and over and over again in my life and that is why I succeed."

♠♦♦♣

HAVING FUN = WINNING ♦

I feel like I'm stating the obvious, but I am. The more fun you have, the more you win. Don't believe me? Just ask Daniel Negreanu. You see him all the time playing poker and he always has a smile on his face, laughing about everything said around him. Of course, he really is having fun, but he is also making sure the players around him are at the same level of comfort as he is. If the table is quiet, mad or unhappy with themselves, then they tend to play a different style than they normally would. They're not relaxed and highly intense about the actions around them as well as the action of their plays. In any situation, it's always more fun and more successful when you and the players around you are more relaxed and having a good time. Players don't realize this, but it's a lot easier to win money against a fun crowd, then it is against am unhappy or mad crowd.

When you're having fun, you're more relaxed and you're able to make easier decisions without straining yourself too much, since the flow of decision-making is a friendlier one. Of course, once the fun goes away, so do your chips (possibly). At this point you will be on tilt and will indirectly lose most, if not, all your chips, unless you can make your opponents go broke first. So you must start out having fun, even if you're not exactly in the happiest mood. It's your job to win as much money as you can, so if you have to act to be happy - to win, then do it. It's better to be naturally happy, because it makes the game that much easier, but from time to time, you may be acting (this usually happens during the "grinding" period), and not just in the cards you play in comparison to the strength or weakness of them.

A friendly "happy" game is the best place to win money at. Just like in your home games, the pace and style of everyone is more relaxed and a joy to be with, decisions are made quickly, players tells are more visible and players normally play softer when the environment around them is uplifting. All of this will result in a victory, if you're on your "a game" and make the right adjustments and decisions against the proper opponents. At the end of the night (in a friendly game), most players will not be mad about losing, but emphasizing more on how much fun they had. For example, listen to the people who go to the casino just to have fun. They may have lost, but they're more focused on the amount of fun they just experienced. It's entertainment value, not financial disasters.

In a game where there are unhappy people, or people who are just quiet and/or mad in general, it will be a little harder to win their money. They play tight, stubborn and their decisions will made through longer levels of thought. The game won't flow freely, which in return will result in less likely a victory. If you're playing your best and making the right decisions, then you still should come out a winner, but quite often, you'll experience more losing sessions then winning sessions at a table with unhappy people, since their unhappiness could rub off on you.

So remember, the next time you play at a poker table, to always be happy and joke around with people. Make them laugh or just join in on the smiles. You'll be surprised how easier the game will be with a table of happy people. Play your best and have fun, because in the end, your bankroll will experience a level he/she is not used to; by having fun at the same time you're playing seriously (in disguise).

And let's not forget, people enjoy playing against happy people. Not too many people like to play against players who argue, yell and insult people. You want to create an image of a player who is friendly, so that those players (hopefully the weaker ones who foolishly throw away their money) will return to your table. It just might be the easiest and quickest way to be rich.

♠♦♥♣

Lancey, The Cincinnati Kid:

"For the true gambler, money is never an end in itself. It's a tool, like language or thought"

♠♦♥♣

TALKING LESS AT THE TABLES ♣

Talking less at the tables will actually help you become more of a winner. A lot of times a player talking out loud about what their opponent is holding or acting on the strength or weakness of their own hand about whether or not they should call (and this process usually takes awhile, while unconsciously giving away vital "tells"). You hear the saying all the time:

"WHEN YOU THINK LONG – YOU THINK WRONG"

Players feel, if you think too long, then you're decision will be wrong. Of course, it is okay to think long quietly to yourself if you're trying to put together a story of what exactly your opponent is holding. Sometimes the best decisions are made when you take your time, but if you take too long your story may be confusing and you might end up making the wrong decision.

This is something I will explain more about later in this book.

Usually when a player talks out loud about what their opponent may be holding, he is pretty much telling him that he is not going to raise (unless he is known to display this act as a tell of strength), and will either fold or just flat call. A lot of times, in this situation, that player will fold. They will put him on a hand that has him beat and will quickly fold, which could have been, the winning hand.

If you can talk to yourself through this situation mentally, you're able to make a better decision, without giving off any information on that opponent or about your own hand. When you speak out loud about what he is most likely holding (all while explaining the story), then you're displaying the type of player he is as well as how he played that particular hand, inadvertently settling on only one decision you can make (the more common one: folding) and giving away information on how that opponent plays. In that same example, you'll also be giving away "tells" about your own hand.

By doing so, you just gave away valuable information that now everyone at the table has gained. By keeping it to yourself, you can make an easier decision the next time a similar situation like that comes up again as well as hiding the value of your own hand.

Don't give away information (or a "tell") about that opponent to anyone. You earned that information on your own and will use it every time you have a chance to. That's easy money, if you think about it. Also, by giving away your own "tells", you'll be giving your opponents an opportunity for easy money against you, unless you can recognize this in future hands and are able to mix the "tell" up against them for your advantage.

Any time you talk at the table about your hand, his hand, the situation etc, you're giving vital information to others at your table. That's information they can now use against that same opponent (or against you). If you talk about the situation at hand, while including your hand, your opponents will see that every time you act, talk or display that kind of information, they will see it as strength or weakness (depending on the result of the hand). It's okay to talk about other things, but never talk about anything relating to the opponents still involved in the hand. Keep all information, tells and decisions in your head. Speak with your actions so that no one around you picks up any new information.

Every time you sit at the poker table try to avoid talking when:

1. You have a tough decision.

2. You're looking for a "tell."

3. You might raise when you know you have a weaker hand, sensing your opponent may fold.

4. You're putting together the story on his game. What did he do pre-flop, flop turn or river.

5. Other players are involved in a hand and you're not.

6. New information is discovered, like finding a new "tell".

7. Someone is trying to gain information on you.

8. You're not that good at hiding your "tells."

9. You're on tilt or on a losing streak. You've been catching bad beats or you haven't been catching any good starting hands. If players around you know you're on tilt or having a bad day, they might use that against by bullying you around.

10. You're involved in any poker hand. Keep quiet until the hand is over and don't expose any information. Joke around, laugh (not at the loser) and overall just display that you're having fun. Like I discussed in the previous section: we all know (now) that having fun equals winning, and you can't be too successful if information is being tossed around like air.

♠♦♣

Jim Rohn:

"Life is a unique combination of "want to" and "how to" and we need to give equal attention to both."

♠♦♣

ADVANCED POSITION ♠

We all know that position is important in any poker game. And I'm sure by now; you know what position is all about, so I shouldn't need to explain too much about this subject (mainly the basic aspects of it). In my first book, I explained a lot about position, but if you're unfamiliar with it, then you should refer to that book. This book is about advanced concepts and not too much basic stuff will be covered. But just in case you need some refreshing, here are some basic positional concepts.

1. Early position: Used for monster hands

2. Middle position: Normally used with strong hands.

3. Late Position: Known for weaker hands.

4. Button/Blinds: Center for bluffing.

5. Position Disadvantage: Acting first, whether there was a raise or not.

6. Position Advantage: Last to act on every round.

7. Bluffing: Players are known to bluff more often in later position.

8. Not Bluffing: Rarely will a player bluff from an early position.

9. Reading a Hand: Position is a great tool to inform you what your opponent is most likely holding.

10. Tells: Positional tells are displayed when position is a factor.

NOW FOR SOME ADVANCED CONCEPTS ON POSITION.

In this section, we will be talking about advanced concepts in position when it comes to a rookie, an amateur and a professional.

Rookie

A rookie will play position more obvious than anyone else at the table. His/her plays will be obvious to what they are holding every time they play a hand, and his defense against position will not exist. You can use position against a rookie, but they won't be able to use it against you. They will fail to see your raise from first position as strength, while you can see their first position raise as a big pocket pair or Ace-King.

When a rookie player plays a hand from an early position, he has strong hand. When he plays a hand from a middle position he is also holding a strong hand, but his requirements may decrease. He may be raising with a hand that he wouldn't play from an early position, but still strong enough to play, like K♥-J♣ or A♦-7♠. When he plays a hand from a late position, then his requirement decrease as well, but roughly stays within his limits (any pair, any ace or any face card). He may play an ever weaker hand, but the majority of the time, all his hands will be strong, or at least suited.

He will be playing any pocket pair, any ace, any suited cards and most likely any 2 face cards. His position when he plays these hands will be the following:

1. He is not bluffing at all from an early position.

2. He is most likely not bluffing from a middle position.

3. He rarely bluffs from a late position, but from time to time, he may pull the "bluff trigger."

You can always tells that position is not in a rookie level players' game. He only plays his hands and not his position or the position his opponents are in. Playing against a rookie, should be easy. When he checks he has a weak hand, when he bets he has a strong hand and when he raises he usually has the nuts, or close to it. From time to time, a rookie level player may pull a bluff or even a semi-bluff, but don't get too attached to that, he may not realize what play he is making nor does he realize that position is a factor in his decision. On the rare occasion a rookie may check-raise. This is a sure sign of a strong hand and folding really is your only option.

Amateur

When an amateur plays a hand from different positions, his starting hand requirements are similar to a rookie level player, only with an amateur, he will sometimes play hands outside his normal list and will occasionally play a hand he has never played before. He will gradually play a hand a rookie level would never play in any position: unsuited connectors, medium kings and queens and rags.

The starting hands that an amateur plays will be the same as a rookie level player: almost any ace, any pocket pair and any high suited connector or face cards, majority of the time. Of course, when an amateur plays these hands, he sometimes looks at everyone's position. He normally just plays his hands in hopes of catching a big pot. He may know about position, but will act less on them than a professional and a little more than a rookie would. The big difference between a rookie and an amateur is their overall level of talent on the felt; being able to make better decisions. Here are some examples.

1. A rookie will play his cards all the time. An amateur will play his cards most of the time. The other times he will play his opponent.

2. A rookie will fail to see position when playing offense or defense. An amateur will play position most of the time. Occasionally he may overlook position and just play his hand,

especially if the pot is large or he feels his hand is worth playing.

3. A rookie is most likely a tight player and will check when he is weak and bet when he is strong. An amateur has the ability to mix it up from time to time, but for the most part will play his hands straight up.

4. A rookie will rarely adjust his game to his opponents. As a matter of fact, a rookie will almost never adjust his game to his opponents, whereas an amateur will occasionally adjust his game to his opponents.

These are some differences between a rookie and an amateur. Of course there are many more differences between them, but we won't get too detailed in all of them, just a few. I just wanted to name a few, so you'll have clearer understanding on how each level differs, but let's get back to their differences in position.

When it comes to position, an amateur has a pretty good understanding on how to play it and how to defend against it. The reason they are considered an amateur is that they don't have the necessary tools to become a professional. Sure, they can be successful, but they will never get to the level of a pro without hard work, more time/experience at the tables and most importantly, the right skills on and off the table, to maintain their money and earn more. They also fail to make correct decisions (consistently), tough calls based on reads and even better folds (which is similar to a rookie). In time an amateur can play as well as a professional. Even a rookie can be on that same page, but there are steps in becoming successful in poker as a professional. You always start as a rookie, fly by as an amateur and if you're determined enough, finish strong as a professional.

Here are some of the different position hands an amateur would play.

1. In early position an amateur will play any pocket pair as well as any ace. He will most likely not play most suited cards or non-connecting face cards, and is smart enough not to bluff from an early position. He knows not to make that mistake, which could cost him a lot of money in the end.

2. In middle position an amateur will play any pocket pair, any ace and almost any suited cards and face cards. Since an amateur "somewhat" knows about position, he'll "sometimes" see who entered before him as well as who is waiting after him. He may fold a normal starting hand if the players before or after him did - or - was - about to make a move. Bluffing is always an option when an amateur plays a hand from middle position.

3. In late position an amateur will play almost any hand, especially if no one has entered

before him. He will most likely enter with a raise with any 2 cards (especially on the button) and will use his position in defense when the flop rolls out. Look out for bluffs. An amateur is capable of bluffing from a late position. In late position an amateur can make a similar play as a professional, but the professional will out play him post-flop.

Now that we had a quick run through on an amateur player, now lets' focus on the king of kings: THE PROFESSIONAL. Let's see how his position skills differ from a rookie and an amateur.

Professional

Here's where you want to be: A level of pure success, a level where position is known to you like the back of your hand. You know how to play position, you know how to defend against position and you know how to mix it up against different opponents in and out of position.

There really is not a whole lot I can say about a professional and his talents, when it comes to position. Most likely he knows it all. When you're in position and make the obvious play, he knows what you're holding. When he is in position and make any play, you probably do not know what he is holding. That's why he is successful, that's why he is a professional, because he knows about position and he knows when to adjust his game to yours when it comes to position plays. Hell, he even knows when to make the proper adjustments no matter what position you or he is in. A professional is capable of making a position mistake, but he'll make them less often than a rookie or an amateur would.

Normally:

1. When you raise from an early position, you have a strong hand. Of course he may not believe you If you're loose player. *And a professional is capable of raising in early position with rags.*

2. When you raise from a middle position, he knows you probably have a good hand. Again, he may not believe you if you're a loose player or the type of player to use middle position to your advantage. *A professional could raise in middle position with any two cards.*

3. When you raise in late position, you may be bluffing and a professional may play back at you. You may get a re-raise at you, but you may just get a call. If he knows what kind of player you are, which I'm sure he does, then he might be setting a trap. Professionals are good at that. They are also better at outplaying their opponents post-flop. Be careful, that could be your last hand. *A professional raising in late position can raise and re-raise with any two cards.*

When it comes to all 3 of these factors, a professional will make a play based on player knowledge, not only who is making the play, but the players waiting to act.

Play cautiously against a professional. He knows about position and can read your hand solely by that. He may also be able to read your hand by other things like: your chip stacking tells, bet sizes, posture, body movements etc. Offensive and defensive position to a professional is like breathing. They know all about it and can do it without thinking. Professionals can make great reads by it alone, but they make most of their money by reading their opponents. They can almost look past your soul and see the cards you're holding. It can be scary. So learn everything you can about position and the rest of your abilities to read different situations and opponents will follow along right behind it.

I'm telling you, making calls by just your opponents' position alone, will shock and amaze you. Too many players fail to see position and all its angles. They focus too much on their own cards and what's in the pot. On many occasions, you'll see how if you would have seen your opponent's position and how he played it, you would have made a different decision; probably a decision that didn't cost you your whole bankroll.

♠♦♦♣

William Joseph Slim:

"When you cannot make up your mind which of two evenly balanced courses of action you should take - choose the bolder."

♠♦♦♣

DO THE OBVIOUS ♥

Most of poker, is playing a hand where your opponent has no clue on what you're holding. On some occasions though, you will have to play a hand where everyone at the table knows exactly what you're holding, and the reason behind that is to protect your hand against outdraws, usually with a pot that is larger than normal, to assure yourself the win.

A play like this is not a normal move to display, but when the situation calls for it, then you must play your hand to a point where it's almost like you're telling your opponents what you're holding. The pot is larger than normal and you need the win because either: the blinds are about to increase or you're trying to gain back some of what you lost earlier in that particular cash game.

A hand that you would normally play in this situation is when you there is a raise and re-raise pre-flop and you hit top pair. You know your opponent does not have an over pair or better, but you don't want him to chase for a card that would put him in the lead, so you play your hand obviously. For example, you have A♦-K♥ and the board is A♣-10♥-9♠. You feel you're opponent may have a weak straight draw or a pocket pair, like Jacks. By playing your hand obviously, you're eliminating the risk of being outdrawn. The pot is big enough to take down, so no need to risk more against an opponent who may get lucky on the turn or river. Sometimes winning what's already in the pot is good enough. Of course, you always want to win more, but in some situations, you need look at it as: a win is a win.

Another situation where playing your hand obviously is when you flop a big hand, like 2 pair or a set. The pot is multi-way and the board shows concern for monster draws (straight and flush possibilities). At this point the pot is probably already large and you want to protect your hand against outdraws (since there are multiple opponents involved in the hand). The correct play in this situation is to raise and re-raise and often as you can. Be aggressive with it on every round to force out the players with their monster draws. Protect your hand and assure yourself that you'll win the pot. You may get callers, but let's hope they miss their draw. If they hit it, you'll know when, when they raise and force you out of the pot. You were unable to protect your hand in that spot, but hopefully next time you'll earn it back.

Playing your hand obviously is also important in a tournament. With the blinds increasing every so often, you need to make sure you have a comfortable stack when entering the bubble and the final table. To get there, of course, you'll need to play your best game as well as getting lucky when it calls for it. You will also need to win the small pots (to help with the blinds) and the pots, where protecting your hand, is the best play. Every little pot/win counts in any game and if you want to make it to the final table and ultimately the first place prize, then you'll need to not only focus on the large pots, but also the pots where you know you have the best hand and protecting it with a large bet or raise.

Throughout a tournament, you'll find yourself in situations where you want to trap by just calling a bet, because you feel you have the best hand and want to extract more bets from your opponent, but that might not always be the best play. Trapping is fine when you have an accurate read on your opponent and the situation allows it, but when your read is not 100% accurate or the pot is large enough, then you'll need to play that hand obviously. Mix up your game and your plays, but make sure you're doing it at the right time against the opponent(s). Slow-playing, trapping and mixing it up is better against a single opponent (maybe against 2 opponents), but when the pot is a multi-way pot and the board is scary, then your only play might be, to playing your hand obviously. Your opponent may read your hand, but that's okay, because you know you'll take down that pot without a fight or any risk at all.

Another part of doing the obvious is betting and raising a hand where your opponents know what you're holding. Your position and bets are obvious to your opponents in comparison to the board shown. For example, the flop rolls out and you hit your pair of aces. You bet out in first position, trying to protect your hand.

Another example is when you hit your straight or flush on the turn and bet out. You are betting to protect your hand against an opponent who could be holding 2 pair or better, based on his information given pre-flop or on the flop.

One more example, is when you hit your much-needed card on the river. You bet out to gain value for your hand. If you decided to check and your opponent checks as well, you might have lost efforts in winning an extra bet. You played the river obvious to your opponent that you just hit your much-needed card, so you're trying to get value for it. He may still call you.

In any one of these situations, a bluff could work. You could try to represent the hand or that you just improved your hand, but make sure you do it against the right opponent.

♠♦♦♣

Dr. James Dobson:

"Great beginnings are not as impor-
tant as the way one finishes."

♠♦♦♣

MIXING IT UP ♦

Mixing up your play is extremely important to do when playing poker at the highest level. When playing against experienced players – like a professional – you'll need to mix up your play at the right times, so they don't have a read on your plays. If you play too obvious and you make similar plays with the same hands, then the more experienced player will pick up on that and adjust their game to make the proper reads, and plays, against it. Of course, if you're involved in a hand with a rookie or lesser experienced player, then mixing it up might not be the right play. Since that player will most likely not adjust his game, by just playing his cards, then your decisions should be easier to make and more straight forward. Play the hand for full value against that opponent and his particular style.

If your table is filled with experienced players, then mixing up your game is crucial, if you want to be successful. Learn when to mix it up. The first time you sit in a game with them, you'll need to really study hard on the plays they are making as well as the plays your making. Understand what moves everyone is making at the table, especially you. Study every move, pick up as many "tells" as you can and most importantly, see what level they play particular hands. See in what situations and positions they bluff, re-raise, slow play etc. Once you've established a high level of skill with all the players at the table, then evaluate what moves you have been making. Have you been check-calling draws, slow playing the nuts, bluffing only when in late positions etc? After some time, you'll understand which players, and what situations, to mix your plays up against.

Most players play a similar style with certain hands. Slow play the nuts, check-raise top pair, 2 pair and sets, bluff in later position etc. The more experienced players know when to mix it up properly at the right times, against the right opponents. If you want to be successful, then you'll have to learn how to do what they (professionals) are doing, by making different plays with similar hands when up against different opponents at different times.

Here is a quick run down on how a professional thinks and how he plays hands differently.

1. **THE NUTS:**

    b. Will check in early position, when a loose player is waiting to act after him.
    c. Will most likely bet in middle or late position with it.
    d. Will only raise with the nuts when he knows his opponent is holding a big hand as well, and the nuts involve 2 cards his opponent would not put him on.

2. **TOP PAIR, 2 PAIR OR A SET:**

    a. Will mix up his betting in early position, depending on the players waiting to act after him. He will most likely check against weaker tight players, and will bet when strong players are waiting to act. Occasionally he will check-raise, if he feels his opponent will most likely call him.

b. Like the nuts, he will most likely bet in middle or late position when holding one of these hands. They may even check if he feels the player(s) acting after him are loose and are itching to bet.

c. Will more often than most bet in late position when holding one of these hands. The only time he might check, is if he feels his opponents are weak and will wait until the turn to bet or raise. He wants his opponents to make a hand (not stronger than his, of course) before he makes his move. On some days, he may even just call on the turn and raise on the river. Knowing his opponent well enough will determine if that is the right play.

3. **THE BLUFF:**

a. Will bluff in almost any position, if he feels his opponents are weak. He may bet in first position, middle position and obviously, late position when bluffing. At any time he feels his opponents are weak he may bet out, hoping to steal the pot. From time to time he may even check-raise with a bluff, if he feels you are bluffing as well. As long as he feels you are weak, he will bluff. No matter what the price is, an experienced player will pull a bluff when his read for your hand – is weak!!

4. **DRAWS:**

   a. A draw can be played in many different ways. Most draws are played with check-calling, while others are played with an early position bet or a late position raise. Defense against these plays can be determined by the player making them. Looser players will bet and/or raise with any draw when the board is showing no concern for a made hand. Tighter players will most likely check-call. A tight-aggressive player will mix it up depending on the players still involved in the hand as well as the what type of action was taken place pre-flop. Weakness pre-flop will result in aggression post-flop. Strength pre-flop, and post-flop will most likely be played soft.

Mixing it up also requires a player to play hands he/she wouldn't normally play; thinking outside the box from their usual starting hands. You will see professionals make this play all the time, simply because, if you only played monster starting hands, your opponents will pick up on that and never give you any action. You must play weaker hands in and out of position if you want to be successful. Make sure when you decide to play a hand you wouldn't normally play (whether with a call or a raise); you must do it against the right opponent(s) at the right time. You must have the skills of a professional and their reading abilities to pull it off successfully at consistent times.

♠♦♦♣

Ryan Sleeper:

"If you can't fold, then you can't win"

♠♦♦♣

TAKING YOUR TIME ♣

Any time you play poker, decisions are being made constantly; whether you take your time or not. Of course, every decision you make will define the success you have on and off the tables. A lot of times, your more important decisions at the table, could cost you you're entire bankroll, so maybe, taking a little more time than usual, might be the best play.

No one is perfect at making the correct decision every time at the poker table, but I think the players who take their time making their decisions will make better and more successful ones more often. I'm not saying to take hours in making a decision, but you must take some time before every major decision you make. Hell, you might as well take your time in every decision you make, but don't take too long on the obvious ones.

For example, if someone goes all in pre-flop and you're sitting there with pocket aces or kings, then it's an easy call with no time to think about it. But if someone makes that same play and you're holding a weaker hand like: Q-9 suited or pocket 5's, then it's not an easy call to make. You must take your time in deciding whether or not your hand is best. You also have to factor in what it will cost you as well as your position in the tournament or cash game. In a cash game it's an easy call when it's only costing you a small percentage, where as in a tournament, it's only a valuable call when it's only costing you a small amount of your chips and you're in position of either making the money (because of your huge chip stack), final table or a spot closer to the first place prize, while already at the final table.

When taking your time at the table, you'll be able to factor in and put together all the information you have gathered from that particular opponent to assure yourself you're making the right decision. You'll be able to put together the story on what your opponent did on every street(if the decision is being made on the river). If you don't take your time in this situation, you might make the wrong choice. You may decide to call or fold based on the "last" information you saw your opponent display. You may see him display a "tell" that represents weakness and instantly call. Not thinking he is acting and is trying to make you call. If you would have taken your time, you might have covered all the angles of his plays and realized that he is actually holding a monster hand.

Taking your time will also help you when you decide to bluff. By taking your time and putting all the pieces of the story together, you may realize that now it's time to bluff. You sense weakness on your opponent and decide to raise, instead of folding, because you knew you were beat and your first instinct in that situation is to fold, where you should have pushed the action by raising. If your opponent is capable of folding a mediocre hand in that spot, then you need to be raising more often.

You will see professionals raise with weak hands against all different kinds of opponents and the reason for this is: that they take their time at the table, when making a decision, and when their story doesn't add up on their opponent as a sign of strength, they decide to make a move and raise. If they only went with their instincts in knowing they are beat and not realizing that if they raise, their opponent may actually fold the winning hand, they could have lost a crucial pot. So, the next time you're at the table, take your time in every decision. You'll be surprised how successful you'll be when doing so - and the decisions you make, are more often correct.

Here are some concepts and strategies that will help you when taking your time at the table.

1. A quick raise usually means strength. By taking your time, you may fool your opponent and play it off as being weak.

2. You know you're beat, so you quickly fold. If you take your time and put the story together on your opponent, you may see that he could be weak and fold to a raise.

3. Your opponent is taking his time in making a decision on the river, as he is doing this you're thinking to yourself, "If he goes all in, I have to fold." He decides to go all in and you quickly fold, because that thought process was stuck in your mind and you reacted on it. If you would have not focused on folding,

if he goes all in, then you might have called. If you would have taken your time and figure out that his play might be a sense of weakness trying to force you out, you would have made the correct decision and called.

4. Multiple players involved in a pot and you have a strong starting hand, there is a raise and a re-raise. By taking your time you'll decide what the best decision is. Sometime you may call and sometimes you'll will re-raise all in. Take your time in these situations and figure out what each opponent is holding as well as your position and what you feel they might be putting you on. Also, factor everyone's position post-flop, hoping you'll be acting last. Once the story comes together, you'll find the right decision.

5. A quick call could represent a draw and if the draw misses the turn or river, then if will be easier for your opponent to force you out of the pot, even if you didn't have the draw in the first place, but had middle pair and backdoor outs. In a situation like this, you should still take your time, even with a draw. Don't let your opponents take the pot away from you in spots of false advertising. In some cases, you may take your time with your draw and decide to raise. Your opponent may not put you on a draw in this spot and if you hit the draw, you might get paid off. Of course, if you

miss the draw, you'll have a better chance of stealing the pot, because your opponent will not put you on that particular hand (the draw).

6. A quick check could easily represent a weak hand or rags. Instead, you should be taking your time even when you miss the flop completely. You never know, you may be able to steal the pot with a raise or a bet on the turn.

♠♦♦♣

Unknown Poker Player:

"Poker is all about timing. It's not about catching pocket aces. It's about catching pocket aces the same time your opponent picks up pocket kings.

♠♦♦♣

PLAYING RAGS LIKE THE NUTS ♠

Playing rags like the nuts is crucial in winning No Limit Hold'em games. If you only play the nuts as "the nuts," then your opponents will pick up on the fact that you only raise and re-raise with the nuts. You're playing your hand like the nuts, so you must have the nuts every time you play you make that aggressive play. Of course, catching the nuts is slim pickings, but when you do, you must play it for full value. I know, everyone knows that by now, but I just wanted to remind you of that, in case you forgot.

When you have a hand that is not the nuts (any hand lower than the nuts) and you feel you can win the hand by playing it like the nuts, then you must play it with full aggression. You apparently have a read on your opponents for either weakness or you sense that they feel you have an extremely strong hand; like the nuts, and you feel if you play it strong, like the nuts, then you'll most likely take down the pot without a contest. My advice is: go ahead and do it. If you feel or sense your opponent is putting you on the nuts, then you must play it as the nuts. Don't back down at all and definitely don't show them your hand afterwards. Let them think you had the nuts. Trust me; it'll be an easier game once you have that power.

In order to play rags like the nuts, you must play it the same way as you would, if you really did have the nuts (which are normally played on the river). Make the same movements, the same size bets and play it the same way as having the nuts; whether you are aggressive with it the whole way or you always slow play the nuts, by check-calling or check-raising.

No matter what your style is, play your rags as if though you have the nuts. But don't play every hand like this or your opponent will pick up on this. Pick your spots when making a play like this. Wait until you're in a situation where it's the best play to win the pot. Think about all the angles of what your opponent is holding as well as what your opponent thinks you're holding. If the story adds you, then it's time to play your rags like the nuts.

Here are some situations where playing rags like the nuts work:

1. Check-calling the whole when there are two of the same suits on the flop. The third suit hits the river and you either bet or check-raise. Doesn't matter what you're holding, when you have a correct read on your opponent and you know he will fold, when trying to represent the flush.

2. When you represent a set or 2 pair on the flop, by raising or check-raise and they know you only do that with 2 pair or better. The river pairs the board and you play it like a full house.

3. Open-ended straight draws on the flop and you call the whole way (like a flush draw). The river completes a possible straight and you now become aggressive with it.

4. Showing aggression on the flop. The turn and river are blanks and you continue to show aggression. No possible straights, flushes or better and you raise or check-raise.

♠♦♣

Unknown Author/Player:

"The guy who invented poker was bright, but the guy who invented the chip was a genius."

♠♦♣

KNOWING WHEN YOU'RE BEAT ♦

If you know you're beat, then the clear choice to make is to fold. If there is no other option, then you have to fold, no matter what is in the pot already or the price of the bet. A lot of players will call a bet, from any street, knowing they are beat or lacking the skills to take to know when they're beat and end up losing a lot more than they expected to. I don't care if the pot odds are great, I don't care if you already put half your stack in the pot. If you know you're beat, and you can't force your opponent(s) to fold, then you simply have to FOLD your hand.

How do you know if you're beat? It's easy! You should already know by now how each of your opponents play. If they make an obvious play of strength, then you know you're beat and your only option is to fold. If you don't how your opponents are playing, then you need to play extremely tight until you have a good understanding on how each opponent plays every hand, in every situation. If you are reading this book, then you should know how to read an opponent, adjust your game to theirs and if there is new information (or a new opponent), then you should already know what to do. If you're not at that level, then you must proceed to the list below for situations where you're most likely beat.

1. When a tight player (or anyone close to it) re-raises pre-flop, you know he has a very strong

hand. This type of player is only playing his/her cards and unless you have a big pocket pair, or maybe A-K, you should be folding. Occasionally you may call when you have position on him and you know exactly how he plays the flop when he hits it and when he misses it. When a tight player re-raises, he most likely has a high pocket pair, aces or kings. He may have queens or A-K, so unless you can beat that, you should be folding. This rule doesn't apply if you know for a fact you can outplay him post-flop, because he plays post-flop softly.

Too many players will call a re-raise pre-flop with A-Q, A-J, A-10 or any pair smaller than 10's and wind up losing to a better hand. Sometimes they will get lucky and outdraw the person, who re-raised them pre-flop, but chances are, most of the time, they end up losing. They see a good starting and are afraid to fold to a re-raise against the obvious player. Like I mentioned in the first section, "Afraid to Fold," you should never be afraid to fold when you know you're beat, especially when you're out of position and your opponent (who is most likely a tight player) is going nowhere.

2. When someone makes a raise from first position and a player re-raises him. You are waiting to act. If you hold anything less than a big pocket pair, then you should be folding; pocket Jacks all the way down to pocket 2's.

You should also be folding A-K all the way down to A-2 as well. Any other hand: easy fold. The player in first position is raising with a big hand. The player who is re-raising knows his opponents position and is raising with a big hand as well. Maybe even a bigger hand. Don't waste your money trying to get lucky against two opponents, who obviously, have strong starting hands.

3. Someone raises pre-flop and bets out on the flop. You decide to raise with top pair with two or more opponents waiting to act. Both of them call and the original bettor re-raises. Chances are your top pair is no good. He is raising not only your hand, but the players who called before him. The pre-flop raiser probably has an over pair, if not, a set. Don't be afraid to fold your top pair.

4. No raise pre-flop and the flop gives you either a flush draw or a straight draw (gut-shot or open-ended). You are last to act and there is a bet, a raise and a re-raise all in. Even though you have a draw that will most likely win if you catch it, you have to fold. The action on the flop indicates that someone has at least 2 pair and at least one other person, could have a draw, while the third person probably has top pair (maybe something stronger). Any way you see it, you're beat (except for the player with the draw). No need to risk your

bankroll on a draw, when you know you need cards to improve in a multi-way pot, where your chances of winning are slim.

5.   When a player shows aggression with multiple players still waiting to act and you're in the middle of it with a mediocre hand. You obviously know you're beat, so fold. The player being aggressive knows there are still many players waiting to act, so his aggression is a clear indication of strength, so fold your middle pair, or gut-shot draw.

6.   You raise pre-flop with a big pocket pair (aces or kings), you get 3 callers and you're last to act post-flop). The flop rolls out and the player in first position bet, while the player in middle position raises. The board is kind of scary so it's probably best to fold. I've seen this many times against the raiser who flopped 2 pair. Sure, you can outdraw him, but you know you're beat, so you fold. I remember raising with pocket aces in this same spot. Same scenario happened and I ended up folding. After the river was completed, I was right, naming the post-flop raiser in having 2 pair. I would have lost. The person in first position only had top pair and ended up losing his whole bankroll.

7.   When a tight player is involved in a hand, whether he shows aggression or not, you

know he has a big hand. Unless you have a big hand yourself or a monster draw, you know you're beat and should fold (or play passively if the tight player is in the flow of action). I see a lot of players call a tight player down to the river or call the tight players bets to the river and end up losing. Didn't they see that the tight player wasn't going anywhere and probably has you beat? I don't care if it's pre-flop or post-flop, when a tight player is involved and the center of the action, you know he has a hand and your only wise choice to make is to fold. Quit trying to see flops against him with a weak hand and quit trying to push him out. He has a hand, he is not going any where, so save your money and make a check-fold play against him.

8. When someone check-raises your bet. We all know that 99% of all check-raises mean: strength (especially at a full table or multi-way pot), so why are we calling with mediocre hands? Why can't we just fold? We know we are beat and why call a raise, when the chancing of winning is slim to none? Knowing your players will help you determine if his check-raise really means strength, but for most players, a check-raise will always means strength.

9. When a player is known for making continuation bets, now decides to check the

flop. Guess what? He is slow playing his hand. He just hit a monster flop and wants you earn as much as he can with it. If you can recognize this, then you should be checking as well. You know you're beat, so don't bet into him. Check it down until he bets, then fold. And unless you improve your hand drastically, you shouldn't be trying to bet into him. Same rule applies if a player is known for the opposite style.

10. Anytime a player plays a different style than he is normally known for playing. Aggression, slow-playing etc, may all mean strength when it's a different style than what you're used to seeing him play. He may be setting a trap or showing aggression to protect his hand. Either or, you're beat and you should check it down or fold. Most players play the same way no matter what, but if a player is confusing you on his particular play, then he might just be setting you up for a disaster. Don't fall into it, just fold.

11. When a player limps pre-flop, a player acting after him decided to raise, then when it comes back to the limper, he re-raises. Too many players who make the original raise will call this players re-raise, not realizing that the re-raiser is sitting there with pocket aces. Occasionally, this player may have pocket kings or even A-K, but the average player will

most likely have pocket aces. In most cases, you will be out of position so why make the call with a hand you know is beat?

Sometimes, you'll have to call a bet or raise when you know you're beat. The pot odds could be tremendous, your outs are high or you have position on everyone with a hand that (or some other reason like, you're feeling it) and if you hit it, it could guarantee a win. Most of the time, when you know you're beat, you must fold. Don't be afraid to fold any big hand when you sense strength from any opponent. That fold could save you a lot in the end. It may seem like a big hand, but if you know you're beat or other factors weight in, then your only choice is to: FOLD.

Knowing when to fold will be determined if you study your opponents' game as well as putting the story together before making any decision. If the story adds up to strength, then it's an obvious fold. If the story doesn't add up, then your opponent could be bluffing. Know the difference and you will, almost always, know when you're beat.

♠♦♦♣

Unknown Author/Player:

"If, after the first twenty minutes, you don't know who the sucker at the table is, it's you."

♠♦♦♣

MOVING UP ♣

Moving up entitles, when a player, like yourself, is ready to move up to a bigger game with bigger blinds and of course, better players (I'm talking about cash games, by the way).

To make this move, you must have an extending amount of experience at the levels below it and you must be successful at all of them. If you're about to start playing a $5-$10 No Limit Hold'em cash games, then that means all the levels below it ($4-$8, $3-$6, $2-$4 and $1-$2) are games where you have been successful at for some time now. These games below the level you are about to play are easy games to you; easy money, and are at a point where it's boring with no competition. With that in mind, you now decide to play a level you are not used to not only win more money, but to gain higher experience.

To make this transaction successful, you must slowly move up into the bigger game. You should know by now, that every level has its own set of players that you must adapt to. It may seem like an easy move, but each level is its own game by itself. Continue to play the lower level, while gradually making the move to the bigger game. Never rush into the bigger game without experiencing what the game is all about. Of course, each table is different at this new level, so take as much time as you can before making the ultimate and semi-permanent move. Once you have established a comfortable understanding on how the new level of players are playing, then it's time to make that level you're new "home." A place you always go to, to win. Occasionally, you may go back to the lower levels game to earn some extra money, especially if you've had a losing day at the new level.

Tournaments are a different story. When you decide to play in a bigger tournament, it just means your bankroll can afford it. Never play a tournament with a buy in bigger than you're used to with a bankroll that is lower than normal. Meaning: don't risk more than you can afford. If you're a regular tournament player you should know when your bankroll can afford a bigger buy in. If you're a regular cash game player and are somewhat new to tournaments, then begin playing smaller tournaments until you have a good understanding on how one plays out.

All in all, it's about comfort when playing a game or level you're not used to. Make your skill level and your bankroll is sufficient enough to make the move. Never completely stray away from the lower levels you're used to. It may be boring to you, but it's the right level for making easy money.

♠♦♥♣

Mark Twain:

"There are few things that are so unpardonably neglected in our country as poker. The upper class knows very little about it. Now and then you find ambassadors who have sort of a general knowledge of the game, but the ignorance of the people is fearful. Why, I have known clergymen, good men, kind-hearted, liberal, sincere, and all that, who did not know the meaning of a "flush." It is enough to make one ashamed of the species."

♠♦♥♣

MOVING DOWN ♠

Moving down is obviously just the opposite of the previous section on moving up. If you're playing at a new level you're not used to, and your success rate is not increasing, then you need to move down into a game where you're more comfortable at as well as a level you can win more consistently at. Also, if you're losing more than you can afford, then a move down might be your best play. You know you can win at the lower levels, so why not go back and win what you lost at the higher level? I'm not saying you'll win every time, but at least you'll be a level where you'll have more confidence in winning.

Everyone wants to move up into bigger games with bigger blinds, more experienced players and of course, bigger payouts (whether it's a tournament or cash game). But like I mentioned in the previous section, it's only good to move up when your skill level and bankroll can afford it. If you're not ready to make the move, then stay where you're at or move down to an even easier game. If you're making money consistently at the lower games, why not just stay there until your bankroll is overflowing? No need to move up into a bigger game and risk it all, when you're making good money where you're at now. In time you'll move up, but for now, stay where you're at. And don't be ashamed to move down to a game where you know you can win practically every time. You're there to make money, so why not make it as easily as you possibly can?

♠♦♣

Jackie Robinson:

"Baseball is like a poker game. Nobody wants to quit when he's losing; nobody wants you to quit when you're ahead."

♠♦♣

TRAVELING ♥

When most people think about playing poker for a living, they don't think about "all" the cost it will take to be successful. Sure, they think about the millions of dollars they "could" win at the poker tables, but they usually ignore all the expenses it takes to even start the professional level process. Everything they need to bring with them to all the tournaments and cash games around the country, if not the world, aside from the buy-ins..

When it comes to be successful in poker, you not only have to have the skills it takes to be successful at the tables, but also the skills away from the tables and the "money" skills it takes to take you there; like money management. (Something I explained a lot of in my first book). It's also money to provide you with the right amount for food, shelter and any other personal needs and wants, but most importantly, it's for all your traveling expenses.

All expenses explained can be spent with a little amount of cash (all except maybe, shelter), but by far the most expensive of it all, would have to be the traveling expenses. Expenses like, your plane tickets. You can find shelter for a cheap price, if not for free, if you have a friend(s) that lives near these extravagant places or a cheap hotel, if you plan to stay there for only a short period of time. Food, clothing and other personal expenses can also be provided at a low cost, but there is no way around the price of a ticket. Sure, you may get discounts from time to time, but ultimately you'll be paying a lot for each trip you take.

Staying at one casino to play poker is a recreational way to play poker, but if you want to be successful and run among the elite, then you'll have to pay your way around the world at whatever cost it takes to bring you there. Not everyone lives in Vegas, so you might want to think about saving a little on the side after each game for travel expenses, gearing up for the WSOP. All while not ignore the other expenses and the price of sitting down at felt.

Sometimes, you'll have to hold off on traveling to bigger tournaments or cash games until your bankroll is bigger. No need to rush it, when you're not ready. Take your time and build your bankroll as sufficient as you can. In time you, with hard work and determination (and some luck), you'll find your way to all the big games around planet earth.

Let's not forget, traveling is not that much fun; going from plane to plane, dealing with luggage and airports and obviously the long rides to each casino game or tournament around the world. Sure, the scenery and experiencing different states and countries are thrills on its own, but getting there is the worst part. Anticipation is great, but after a while it's redundant.

Sometimes, just playing locally, while making the trip just to the WSOP, might be the best way to make a living; though it's not always the most enjoyable way to play poker at the highest level. Professionals travel all around the world to all these high end tournaments and cash games, so maybe you should follow in their footsteps. If that's not possible, then don't worry, you can do quite well playing in local places.

♠♦♦♣

Lou Krieger:

"Most of the money you'll win at poker comes not from the brilliance of your own play, but from the ineptitude of your opponents."

♠♦♦♣

TELEVISION EXPOSURE ♣

Television exposure is something everyone in this world wants. It makes them feel famous. And what better way to be famous, then to be on television playing your favorite game at a chance to win millions of dollars?

Professionals, you see on television, are pretty much used to being in the spotlight, but what about the new players that comes along and win their first televised tournament? Think they can handle being the center of attention? Some might, while others aren't able to. If you know you're going to be on television, you might start out being nervous and probably make some donkey plays, but that's okay, it's natural. What you have to do, while at the table, is to ignore everything that is going on around you. Focus on the table and the players around you. Act like it's a home game with some friends, in the distant, watching you. Ignore the cameras and all the hype that surrounds it. You made it that far, why blow it because your nerves took over your ability to succeed?

After a short while, I'm sure your nerves will calm down and you'll start playing your "a game." Even though you're on television, you can't be afraid to make tough folds and even tougher plays, like raising or re-raising an opponent with rags. You're there for a reason: to make the most money and the first place prize. Of course, to win it all will be extremely difficult given the fact that everyone else at the table has that same goal. All you can ask for is to play your best. Listen to your instincts, discover new information on every opponent and make the plays, you feel, are best for the right situation. If you can focus entirely on the players and the game at hand, you should have no problem adjusting to the television exposure.

Some players use the crowd to their advantage, while others ignore the crowds completely. Whether style you have, use it. Do whatever you feel is best for the action and reaction at hand. You're only real goal is to win the tournament. So, while the cameras are on, play the game you love and let's hope you won't get unlucky and fall short of the 1st place. But if you do come up short, then all I can say is, "You played your best and now all you can do is to chalk it up to experience. You had fun, you were on television and you won some money. Next time will definitely be different, you'll be more comfortable at the table, with all that hype, and walk away the only player left standing. Hopefully!!

Let's not forget what being on television can bring to your career. Endorsements! Just being on television one time can bring endorsements your way. If they see you are prime material on the table as well a crowd favorite, you just might find a new "side" career endorsing poker websites, clothing, commercials etc.

♠♦♦♣

Chinese Proverb:

"If you must play, decide upon three things at the start: the rules of the game, the stakes, and the quitting time."

♠♦♦♣

FAME AND FORTUNE ♠

Fame and fortune is what everyone in the poker world is trying to accomplish. It's a chance to play a game where you can ultimately be rich and famous from. What better job is there, then playing a game for money? Traveling, meeting new people, playing cards and walking away with hundreds, thousands or even millions of dollars. In my opinion, there is no better job than professional poker player. It's not easy being a professional poker player, but if you're skilled enough on all levels, then it's, by far, the best job in the world.

Like any celebrity, fame and fortune is not easy to accomplish, nor is it easy to deal with. First you must set your skills at a level where you have a chance for fame and fortune. That could take years. Next you must complete a project or tournament where the prize money is higher than normal. Any big tournament where first place is over a million dollars is the right tournament to win. Of course, winning any tournament of any value is nice, but the bigger the tournament, the bigger the fame and fortune. Last, but not least, is being able to handle the fame and fortune, all while continuing your success that once got you there. That last step could be the hardest of them all.

Many new players will play a tournament and win a big prize pool, but they won't necessarily be famous for it. They may have the fortune, but they don't have the fame yet. Anyone can win a tournament, but only the better players will win more often, with the fame and fortune to soon follow. You've established the fortune, but if you want the fame to go with it, then you must continue playing poker and find ways to be successful at it, consistently. Luck is always a factor, but if you work on the skills part of it, you should be able to overlook the level of luck and project yourself in to poker fame. After you win a few tournaments (especially the bigger, more renowned tournaments), your level of fame will increase. Small tournaments are great for easy money, but it won't get you the fame you're probably looking for. Here some quick steps in accomplishing both fame and fortune.

Step one in fame and fortune was your levels of skills on the felt. As this point in your career and the fact you're reading this book, you should already have a set level of skill on the table, so I won't really go into this step. Continue growing as a player and keep doing what you're doing to be successful.

Step two is actually winning a big tournament. If you haven't done so yet, keep playing. Once day you'll take down a major event. The more you play the better chance you have of winning.

Step three is maintaining a certain level of success, all while increasing your wins and the fame portion of it. To increase your fame and fortune status, you must be playing your best at all times, cashing and winning tournaments, being on television a lot with commercials, or just being seen at the tables, being interviewed and etc.

Keep the spotlight on you with your poker skills, not your loud mouth or crazy antics. Focus on your game and always try to play your best. Over time your level of fame and fortune will increase at the same rate as a professional you see all the time on television. We all want to be at that level, so why not do whatever it takes to be there? My ultimate goal is to be rich and famous for my poker skills and I'm willing to do anything to reach it. My skills at the table, my poker books and my continued success are leading me to that level. It may take some more time to be at the same level as a top professional, but I'm willing to do the work it takes to be right next to them. Hell, I'll do whatever it takes to pass them. By the end of my career I want to be known as one of the best poker players ever. Are you determined enough to have that same goal, because I am?

♠♦♦♣

VP Pappy:

"If you ain't just a little scared when you enter a casino, you are either very rich or you haven't studied the games enough."

♠♦♦♣

FAMILY AND FRIENDS ♦

Every poker player out there has friends and family, but not all of them support the career of a professional poker player. In fact, very few friends and family would ever consider their love-ones to gamble for living. In the rare cases out there, there are people who will completely support their friends or family members being a professional poker player. Of course, you will find a lot more support in your friends than your family. And you'll find even less support in most of your family, more importantly speaking about your parents.

Parents raise their kids to have real jobs (most of which require a college degree). They want their kids to assure themselves a good paying career to support themselves and their upcoming family (spouse, kids etc). They don't like the fact that gambling is even an option when it comes to your kid's career. If you're in a situation like this, you must inform your parents that you'll be starting out in small games where your personal assets and financial states will not be effected. You may even want to have a part time job during this process so earn more support over it.

With a lot of skill and time on and off the table, hopefully you'll venture into bigger games. As long as you're doing well, your parents should support you through your status. For the best support, keep them inform on the wins and loses of your career poker bankroll. If they see vast improvements in your bankroll, then you should have no problem increases your stakes, while traveling to major events around your area. In time, you'll eventually travel to all the major events around the country, if not, world, where the support will follow.

As your bankroll and skill increase, so will your support from your family and friends. Let's hope one of your big wins is a televised event. You parents will have no bigger support than seeing you at the final table of a major event, where first prize is over a million dollars. Even in events mildly smaller than the million dollar event, your parents should still give you equal support. Once they know you have a chance of winning enough money to support yourself, your family and even them, they will support you 100%. After that tournament (hopefully after cashing well), your support from your family and friends will remain at its highest level. Now you can play poker full time, quit the part time job and show everyone what a star you are in the poker community. This last step may not be the best decision, but if you're passionate enough about poker, like I am, then you have to take that risk. If you're serious about playing poker for a living, then I know you should have no problem being successful at it.

If your parents, friends and family already give you full support from the beginning of your poker career, then there is nothing special you have to do to earn anyone's support. Simply play your best and hope to do well. Always try to improve your game and play as much poker as you and your bankroll can handle. Make sure you're picking the right games for the best results. Support is not easy to come by, but once you have it, all else is smooth riding – except for those bad beats.

♠♦♥♣

Vince Lombardi:

"We didn't lose the game; we just ran out of time."

♠♦♥♣

MENTAL POKER AND ITS STRESS ♥

Mental poker is extremely important in being successful in poker. Understanding how to handle your money and earn more properly is the key to being a professional - as well as handling the swings every poker player goes through. We all know by now what games to pick and what stakes to play at. We also know when to move up and when to move down, but do we really know all the concepts in mental poker to hang with the professionals? Let's not forget all the stress surrounds it.

To be successful as a professional poker player, you must understand the different levels of mental poker as well as how to maintain its ever changing adaption to the number of players involved and the skill level of every new and old player out there today. Not to mention, the increase of money that exchanges each players hand on the daily basis and the wins and loses each player will go through. These levels are basic (with some intermediate and advanced ideas) and were covered in my first, *The Ultimate Hold'em Book*.

Levels like:

1. Avoiding the prize money and focus on the just playing your best.

2. Keeping records of where you play and how much you win or lose.

3. Picking the right cash game that fits your bankroll and your level of skill.

4. Playing tournaments you have time and money for that meshes well with your style, time available and experience.

5. Learning from past mistakes and avoiding to repeat them.

6. Preventing yourself from going on "tilt."

7. Ignoring the fame and fortune, while at the tables.

8. Treating the game and the players with respect.

9. Understanding your opponent's game at an advanced level.

10. Leaving your ego at the door and no to act on revenge.

11. Ignoring chatter and your personal problems, while at the table.

These are just some of the things I talk about in my first book. These parts of mental poker are extremely important if you want to be successful in poker. If you have already accomplished a higher level of these particular parts of mental poker, then your only goal now is to maintain this level, while playing your best. If not, then read these concepts again or buy my first book for a complete understanding of them and its full complexity.

From time to time you will find yourself stressed out over a losing hand or a losing session, but that happens to everyone. Don't' let these swings affect your play or how you spend your money.

Now, let's focus on the some advanced concepts when it comes to mental poker and its stress.

Whether you're at the table or away, your mental capacities must remain at its all time high. Since you already know how your opponents play, you should focus on other things like, picking up "tells", listening to your instincts, assessing the situation at hand, thinking what hand your opponent is putting you on and etc – all while at the poker table. Once you have put together the complete story of what is going on at the current hand, you should be able to make the right decision more often than most. To keep this level of mental stability, you must constantly being doing your homework (on and away from the table). Focus on the 10 or so players at your table and nothing else. A lot of players will even take notes, while at the table, to make their decisions easier. If you're memory isn't the best, then I would suggest you take a note book to the table with you.

Away from the table is a little easier. It's just the ability to accurately pick the right games and stakes that fit your style and bankroll. Too many players will play outside their limits, because they had a bad beat or a losing session and will try to win it back quickly at

Ryan Sleeper

a higher staked table. This is where most players fail at being successful. If a bad beat or a losing session just occurred, you must maintain the mental part and the stress behind it where its status of that is of a winner. Keep playing that same level or even move down one level. Sometimes walking away and taking a break is the best form of "not" putting yourself on "tilt" and relieving any stress.

Whether you win or lose, you must remain at the level you are most successful at. In time you will move up, but to maintain the highest level of mental poker and its stress behind, you must stay the levels you play the best at. If you're winning money without a fight, you should continue playing at that level. Why let the previous hand, a losing session or an obnoxious opponent take you off your game? You're there to win and play your best, so why let everything else around you effect the way you play? Come prepared and leave you satisfied.

Mental poker and its stress behind it is probably the most important part of being successful aside from the skills it takes to play your cards, your opponents and the board shown. If you can understand and maintain a high level of controlling your mental aspects and stress behind poker, you WILL be successful. I assume your skills on the felt are advanced, so as long as you can handle the stress of wins and loses and all the mental parts of poker, you'll should have no problem being a successful professional poker player.

Another part of stress in poker is luck. Luck is one of the hardest things to deal with, stress wise, in the game of poker. Since you can't control luck, it's virtually impossible to let it not affect you. Everyone in poker will get lucky, and of course, get unlucky. Realizing that everyone has there fair share of luck and being able to let it go (if you get unlucky) will help you out a lot when playing poker successfully.

Understand this: Everyone will get lucky and unlucky an equal amount in their lifetime. The players who understand this and ignore the bad beats will be more successful and less stressful. You win, you lose, you get lucky and you get unlucky, but you must learn that this happens to everyone who plays poker, not just you. Learn to ignore it all and watch how quickly your status as a professional increases. Don't believe me, ask your bankroll.

♠♦♦♣

Nick Seitz:

"The breakfast of champions is not cereal, it's the opposition."

♠♦♦♣

PLAYING TOO MANY HANDS ♣

This is probably the biggest mistake new players to poker make. Even some more experienced players make this mistake as well. Whether you just like action and love to gamble or you've been catching rags all night and now decide to play any decent hand from then on out, you're setting yourself up for an unfortunate result.

Suited cards, any ace or any two face cards may seem like strong starting hands, but unless you understand your opponent's game and position pre-flop and post-flop, you might find yourself losing more than you expect. Raises, re-raises, or all ins are all action moves, but certain hands should not be played under optimal circumstances.

Understanding what your opponent is holding when they raise and re-raise will determine whether not you should playing your weak ace or suited connector. If you're in a situation where you're not sure what your opponent is holding, sometimes folding and watching him/her play it out will inform you on their style, without risking your chips. Once you learn how they play that particular hand, then you can make the proper adjustments the next time you're in a hand with them.

From time to time you may end up folding a good hand, where you may have the won the pot, but that happens. Your read was correct pre-flop, so you made the correct fold. Who cares if you would have won the pot. If you played every hand to a flop, turn or river you will see a lot of exits without pay. You will either: call every raise pre-flop and end up folding on the flop when you miss the hand or you'll call your opponents bets to the river with weak/missed draws or weak pairs and end up losing to a better hand.

You really need to learn how all your opponents play every hand in different situations. It'll make your decisions a lot easier when you're involved with these particular opponents. Learn to fold when you sense you are beat and learn to call, raise or re-raise when you sense weakness or want to extract more money. Like I've talked about earlier in the book about not being afraid to fold, raising when you sense weakness, re-raising with rags and knowing when you're beat, it all covers the skills it takes to be successful, while not playing too many hands that could risk you and your bankroll depressing falls.

Here are some concepts on "playing too many hands."

1. You're in the big blind and there was a small raise in early position. It only cost you a small portion, but it could result in losing all your chips. You're out of position and the raise was from an early position; meaning he probably has a strong hand and unless you hit a monster flop, you'll most likely be folding. Even catching a decent a flop can cost you your chips if your opponent is reeling you in with a trap.

2. You've been catching "any aces", suited cards and face cards and the tables is filled with experienced players and are playing extremely aggressive. Position (acting late) will factor if you should play these hands and the ability to read these opponents and how they play. Early position you should be folding these hands, middle position you should be folding or raising depending on the players acting after you and late position you should be calling or raising with these hands when you read your opponent(s) for being weak. I'm a post-flop player (where I make better decisions after the flop) so I'll make these calls more often to out-play my opponent(s) post-flop, but I wouldn't make the call if I feel my opponent has me dominated. Don't play a hand just because it has a lot of potential or it's only costing you a small portion of your stack. Too many players will play any ace, suited cards and face cards to raises and re-raises and end up losing a lot of pots and money. Only play these types of hands when the situation calls for it. If you sense your opponent for having a better ace, pocket pair or just a better hand overall, then you must fold.

3. Players who love to see flops, because they feel anything is possible, so they call every bet and raise pre-flop hoping to catch a big

flop. 2 out of 3 times, a player will miss the flop; imagine how much you will lose on those missed flops. Even if you hit the flop, you may not make back what you lost in your previous hands.

4. You've been catching rags all night; you finally see a good hand and win with it. Now you decide to start playing more hands similar to the one you just won with. Not a good idea. Now, anytime you catch a decent hand, you'll play it to any bet or raise. This means you're playing outside your level, resulting in playing too many hands and most likely experiencing a lot of early exits and lost money.

5. You have a lot of chips in front of you, due to luck or playing your best. You obviously dominate in chips over anyone at your table, so you decide to play more hands to see how long the rush lasts. Don't be surprised if you end up losing what you just earned. If you're in a situation like this, you must continue playing your game. Don't step out of your style and play hands you wouldn't normally play in those spots.

♠♦♥♣

Jerry Barber:

"The more I practice, the luckier I get."

♠♦♥♣

DO THEY REALLY HAVE IT? ♠

To truly know if someone has the hand they are representing or not, first you must know what kind of player they are. At this point in your career, I'm sure you know the different types of players there are as well as what kind of hands they like to play. You also know which players are capable of mixing it up at the proper times. Occasionally a player may make an unfamiliar play that leaves you baffled, but more often than most; this player will make similar plays in similar situations.

Most plays you make should be made on the flop, while occasionally on the turn. I think all major moves should be determined before the river, though some of your major plays will be made there. These plays will be unwavering by the previous plays your opponent just made prior to the river. If the story doesn't add up, them he most likely doesn't have the hand he is trying to represent.

For example, I remember one time a player limped in early position with no raise after him. The flop rolls out and everyone checks, including me, because I limped in pre-flop as well... with

Q♦-10♣.

The turn comes a blank (5♠) and everyone checks again. I think at this point I had middle/second pair (10's), but didn't want to bet for some reason, I don't remember. Maybe, because there was an Ace on the flop and didn't want to bet out in case someone was slow playing their ace. The river was another low card and this time the player in early position bet 2/3 the pot.

With a board of A♦-3♥-10♦-5♠-2♣,

I didn't think my opponent had a 4, for the straight, giving the fact that he limped in early position and he was considered a semi-tight player. His only possible holdings were pocket 4's or A-4. He wasn't the type of player would limp in early position with Ace-4 or any ace really, because he would have made a bet on the flop or turn with it, so pocket 4's was his only possible holdings. I really didn't feel he had the hand he was trying to represent, so I called his bet and won with my pair of 10's.

Many situations like this will occur where you will have to put your opponent on a few hands he/she could possibly be holding. If you play back what he did pre-flop all the way to river, you should have a good idea of what he/she is actually representing.

Here are some hands different types of players are capable of playing when they play them to the river, especially when everyone is playing the board weak.

Tight player:
Most tight players will represent their hands to a point where you can read them pretty easily. Rarely will they show strength when they are actually weak.

If the board shows concern for a straight or flush (or better), a tight player will most likely check it down if they don't have it. If they do bet, then they probably have the hand they are trying to embody.

Loose player:

A loose player will almost always try to represent a hand they don't actually have, especially if he senses weakness from his opponents. When the board shows concern for a big hand, a loose player will play it aggressively trying to represent that particular hand. Unless you have a good read on them, you'll end up losing a lot of pots where your middle or bottom pair was actually good. Trapping against a loose player is the best defense against this type of play. Calling a loose player more often is a good play when he/she is trying to act as if they have the nuts.

Tight aggressive:

A tight aggressive player will mix it up depending on his position and the type of players still involved in the hand. If he senses weakness or has position, he will almost always try to represent the hand he is ultimately trying to display. If he feels an opponent may have the hand or is acting first on the river, he will less likely try to make a move at the pot with anything less than a high valued hand.

Maniacs:

Maniacs are very similar to a loose player, but are capable of making more plays (with bluffs) in any situation, no matter who is still in the pot. This type of player will constantly make plays where he is trying to represent the hand his opponents are putting him (or anyone else at the table) on. A loose player will occasionally back off from trying to bluff at a board that shows a big hand, where a maniac will rarely ever back off from this state of affairs.

If you're capable of reading your opponents and how they play their hands to the river, then you should have no problem dividing the facts, in situations on whether they have it or not. Put the story together from pre-flop to river and you will have the ability to make calls with weaker hands against opponents who make big bets trying to represent the hand they are betting into.

♠♦♣

Author Unknown:

"Take risks: if you win, you will be happy; if you lose, you will be wise."

♠♦♣

READING OTHER POKER BOOKS ♥

Many players, who play poker these days, don't read poker books. They simply sit down at the table and learn by ear. They hope to get lucky early on and learn everything they can, while experiencing the thrills of it. What they don't realize is that when they sit down, they are only playing their cards and relying on the luck. Sure, they know the rules and what beats what, but unfortunately they don't know the skills or guidelines behind those skills needed to be successful. I know that experience at the table is the best way to improve your game, but if you don't have the basics skills or understandings of poker, then you won't be successful as quickly as you would like it to be.

By reading other poker books, you'll learn all the basics of poker as well as some intermediate and even some advanced ideas on how to be successful. You may not learn everything about everything in poker books, but you will have a good understanding on how to play different opponents in different situations, where the results of being successful will prevail much quicker than someone who has never picked up a poker book.

When I started playing poker, I didn't read any poker books. Hell, I never thought I would ever read a poker book, much less, than actually write a book. Early on in my career, I did quite well in home games (since that was the only place I could play at, being under 21). But I knew if I wanted to be more successful I would have to take bigger risk, play bigger games and of course, find a way to be consistently successful.

After turning 21, I decided to make all the necessary moves it would take to be successful. Improve my skills on every level, including breaking down and buying a poker book. My first book I ever bought was, Doyle Brunson's - *Super System*. I figured if I was going to be the best, why not buy the bible of all poker books, written by the best poker player of all time. As time passed by, I ended buying many other poker books, all while trying to improve my game. I wanted to cover everything I could about basic and some intermediate strategies in poker (mostly Hold'em) so that when I moved up into bigger games as against better players, I was more prepared.

People don't realize that reading poker books will give any new player (and even some more experienced players) a good understanding on how to handle yourself in different situations as well as a new perspective on how that particular author (or the player stated in their examples) plays poker. Not to mention how the average player plays, which there are more of that type than any other.

Poker is all about information, so why not try to extract as much information as you can; watching poker on television, playing poker at the tables and even poker books all have that information. If you want to be successful and be labeled one of the best poker players in the world, then you must obtain as much information as you can about the game of poker and its players. Reading might not be the best form of entertainment, but it will provide you with new information on how to be successful in poker. I wouldn't be surprised if even the seasoned professional finds something new in poker books. I know you'll find something new in this book you haven't thought about before or something you never even knew.

All in all, don't play poker unprepared. Don't think you know everything about poker and how to be successful at it. Learn as much as you can, when you can. Watch, play and read all about poker and I assure you, you will be happy you did. I don't regret buying poker books, but I do regret not buying them sooner than I did. All my poker books have helped in different situations. They have guided me through some tough times and have provided me with some enjoyable forms of entertainment. They have made my transition at the table much easier, and I'm thankful for that.

New information is displayed every day, it's your job to pick up that information and use it to your advantage. Reading a poker book is a great first step in pursuing your poker dream and providing you with some very helpful information.

HERE ARE SOME RECOMMENDED POKER BOOKS I SUGGEST YOU READ:

1. **"Hold'em Poker for Advanced Players"** by David Sklansky and Mason Malmuth. Advanced concepts in limit Hold'em, but similar plays in this book can also be used in No Limit Hold'em.

2. **"Super System"** & **"Super System 2"** by Doyle Brunson (with other professionals). Basic, intermediate and advanced strategies in multiple games, like Limit and No Limit Hold'em, 7-stud, Pot-Limit Omaha, High/low, 5-card draw (though not played professionally), Triple Draw and Online poker.

3. **"The Ultimate Hold'em Book"** by Ryan Sleeper. Basic, intermediate and advanced strategies in No Limit Hold'em cash game and tournaments. A great collection of (almost) all the necessary skills it takes to be successful.

4. The **"Harrington on Hold'em Series"** (cash games and tournaments) by Dan Harrington and Bill Robertie. The ultimate collection in successful strategies in cash games and tournaments. Great step by step form for success in either type of game.

5. **"The Theory of Poker"** by David Sklansky. Advanced strategies and concepts in all forms

of poker. A must have for any serious poker player.

6. **"*Full Tilt Poker – Tournament Edition*"** by professionals that play on Fulltiltpoker.com. Successful tips, strategies and concepts for winning poker tournaments. This book covers all forms of poker and how to be successful in any game.

7. "***Killer Poker by the Numbers***" & "***Tournament Killer Poker by the Numbers***" by Tony Guerrera" Math, odds and statistics on successful plays based on the "numbers" in poker.

8. Alan N. Schoonmaker Collection – "***Your Worst Poker Enemy***", "***Your Best Poker Friends***" & "***Poker Winners are Different.***" A great collection of mental strategies and concepts for any poker player to handle stress, money management, opponent adjustments and so much more. Skills needed to be successful, not specifically relating to the skills it takes to play the game, while on the felt.

9. "***Ace on the River***" by Barry Greenstein. Advanced strategies and concepts for anyone who wants to be successful in the poker world. This book gives you all the perspectives of what it takes to be successful.

10. **"*Power Hold'em Strategy*"** by Daniel Negreanu (and other professional poker players). Successful strategies in Limit and No Limit Hold'em, No Limit Hold'em tournaments and Small Ball strategy.

♠♦♦♣

Charles Lamb:

"Cards are war, in disguise of a sport."

♠♦♦♣

TABLE IMAGE ♦

Table image is extremely important to know when playing against an opponent. Knowing someone's image or style of play they are displaying can help you determine how to play against them in different situations. In my first book, I covered a lot about image and how to use it and defend against it in multiple situations. With this book I want to take a more advanced approach to it. I am going to explain how table image of your opponents will make you successful and unfamiliar plays you wouldn't normally make, you will learn when to make them and by doing so, your results will earn you more money and more wins.

We all know by now what types of players there are and how they play different hands in different positions. We also know about "tells", who is capable of mixing it up, instincts, game situations and board analysis. Now we are going to talk about how a players image, when displayed, can help you make the correct decision against them virtually every time.

Here are some types of styles and how image should be played to your advantage:

TIGHT PLAYER:

You know how a tight player plays. You know he only plays big cards and will only continue to the river if he has a monster hand. His image is displayed all the time, so there really isn't much to say about this except for:

1. Don't bluff against a tight player when you know he has a good hand.

2. Don't make daring raises and re-raises when he is playing a hand against aggressive opponents or he is being aggressive himself.

3. If he raises pre-flop, then give him credit for a big hand and don't try to bully him out of it or call his bet with weak hands, especially out of position.

4. If he is showing weakness, then you must attack the pot with a big bet or raise.

Play your cards (and all opponents) like you would normally play them, but back off when you know the tight player is involved and is either showing aggression or calling bets and raises against opponents who are aggressive themselves.

LOOSE/MANIAC PLAYER:

A loose/maniac player's image is obvious. They play almost any hand in any position. The best play against them is to play tight, but in some cases you need to be even more aggressive than they normally are. Learn to raise and re-raise against them any time you have a strong hand. Occasionally you will set a trap when they choose to be the more aggressive player. The flop is when the loose/maniac player will construct the most action, so waiting for the turn or river, to raise, is a great way to extract more money from these types of players. Picking what cards to play against them will always vary. Of course, you'll play all big starting hands, but from time to time you should be playing weaker hands or even rags against any loose or maniac player. Since you know they will play equal hands in value, you'll be able to dig up more pots and wins when you are more aggressive than them post-flop, on board that has helped your hand. If you feel he may back down by your reads on the value of his hand or position, then you must play weaker hands against them and hope to out-maneuver him on later streets. A loose player will back down when they sense they are being bullied and their hand is valued less than the minimum status of what they would normally call with.

Another thing about playing a loose/maniac player is, you'll be able to make more calls post-flop against them, where as against a tight player you'll make more folds (when he is representing strength). When a tight player bets on the flop, you can put him on at least top pair and if you have middle pair, then you might have to fold. Against a loose player, who bets on the flop, you're more apt to make calls with middle or bottom pair (or even two over cards). A loose player is more capable of bluffing, so making a call with a weaker hand might be the correct play. Same rules apply when playing against either type of opponent on the turn or river.

TIGHT-AGGRESSIVE PLAYER:

We all know playing against a tight-aggressive player is the hardest player to be successful against. His image is the ability to mix it up, so I don't feel I need to explain too much about playing against all players with this label. When playing against a tight-aggressive player, simply play at his level. When the situation calls for it:

1. Mix it up.

2. Set traps.

3. Play certain hands obviously.

4. Raise with weaker hands than you would normally raise with.

5. Re-raise when you sense weakness.

6. Bluff.

7. Listen to your instincts.

8. Make all the proper adjustments you need to make to assure yourself you're making the correct play against them.

This section is mainly for playing against a loose or maniac player. Someone who: bluffs a lot, plays weaker hands in and out of position and is known to want action on every round. Playing against this type of player requires you make plays you wouldn't normally make against other players. Players today will call a big bet or raise on any street against a loose or maniac player (and would probably win the pot with it), because their opponents image is "loose", so they are more comfortable making this play, believing that their opponent is highly likely to be bluffing. Make a play like this against a tighter player may not be the best play. Over your poker career you'll make (or you should be making) a lot more calls against a loose player than you would against a tight player. And I wouldn't be surprised how often you calls were correct. It's a lot easier to make a call when his table image of your opponent is labeled – LOOSE.

One more thing about making calls against a loose or maniac player: If you are showing aggression and he is playing at back you, you must decide if he is actually holding a strong hand. If you feel he has a strong hand, by the way he played it, then you should fold. When a loose player is showing aggression against a player he knows has a big hand, by the level of strength he is playing his hand, then the loose player probably has a very strong hand as well and feels his hand is stronger than yours.

♠♦♦♣

Michael Pertwee:

"How long does it take to learn poker, Dad?" "All your life, son."

♠♦♦♣

PUTTING ALL THE PIECES TOGETHER ♣

Congratulations! You've made it to the end. Well, near the end. A couple more things to talk about and you'll be ready to play against the professionals and actually win money from them - consistently. You'll also be ready to play in your biggest cash game (with a winning session) or a tournament, and as long as you don't get extremely unlucky, you'll be on your way to the final table and in due course of that first place prize. If you have read other poker books, including my first book, then you should have no problem being successful at poker. As long as you continue to do your homework (on your opponents), pick the correct games for your style and bankroll, adjust your strategies properly, handle all the stress of winning and losing and know when to keep playing and when to quit, then you need to start playing poker at levels you only dreamed about playing at.

Now, is your chance to play, against the best, beat the best and walk away with thousands or even millions of dollars. Your face will be on television and your name will be mentioned on a daily basis. But before we proceed to the end of this book and your path to glory, let's talk about what we learned in this book and put all the pieces together.

1. In the first section we talk about no being afraid to fold. I hope, by now, you are capable

of folding any hand at any time. If you sense you are beat and/or out of position, then you should be folding hands you wouldn't normally fold. Never be afraid to fold a pocket pair pre-flop or a big ace, not to mention any hand slightly less in value than the ones previously stated. If you know you're beat and can't force your opponent to fold, then a fold is your only option.

2. Section 2 covers: not raising just because you can. Just because you have a monster chip stack, doesn't mean you should be raising with any hand against any opponent. Pick your spots and your opponents before making a raise.

3. Section 3 covered: not acting on revenge. I don't care if you don't like your opponents or the fact that you just got outdrawn by them with a hand they shouldn't have been involved in, in the first place. Play your game and focus on the next hand. Avoid revenge and avoid tilt, and you should have no problem earning your money back, if your skill level is advanced and the game is running to your advantage.

4. In section 4 we covered: attacking the weaker players. They are easy to read, so why not focus more on winning their money over the

players who are more skilled and know how to mix it up and hide their tells?

5. In section 5 we talked about taking long shots. Not the best idea when the odds are against you. Play more hands where pot odds, and your hand value are more to your advantage. Taking long shots, like a gut-shot draw or chasing for an over card can leave you broke quicker than you can imagine.

6. Section 6 was filled with information concerning about putting your opponent on a hand. This section should be obvious. Whether you're involved in a hand or not, you should always try to put the active players on a hand. Limit yourself to one or two possibly holdings.

7. Section 7 is focused on the theory if bluffing is overrated. Bluffing is a part of the game and you must bluff to be successful, but I think too many people strive more on bluffing and less on reading their opponents. Bluff when the time is right, but focus more on reading your opponents and making the correct decisions against them.

8. Section 8 is all about taking risks. You must take risks when the situation calls for it; late in a tournament or short-stacked in a cash game. Even when you know you're behind

you must take the risk if the price is right and realizing that it's your only option.

9. Section 9 is calling with nothing. Very rarely will you make this play, but when you sense weakness and want to steal the pot on a later street, you must call with nothing (normally on the flop) to bet out on the turn or river knowing your opponent will most likely fold.

10. Section 10 is all about raising when you sense weakness. When you sense weakness from your opponent(s), you must raise, no matter what you're holding. The occasional call might be correct, but more often than most you should be raising when you know your opponents are weak and will most likely fold.

11. Section 11 is: knowing when to re-raise with rags. No matter what you hold, you need to learn when to re-raise with rags. Position and player knowledge will help you determine when the best time to make this daring play. This section goes along with raising when you sense weakness, only this time you can raise with any hand against an opponent, you know, has a good hand and is capable of folding it.

12. Section 12 covers: taking control of the table. Whether it's luck or the image of luck, you can control you table and ultimately force your

opponents to fold hands he/she wouldn't normally fold.

13. Section 13 talks about relying on luck. Just like section 8, you have to (sometimes) put yourself in a situation where luck is the only factor for the win. Luck is there for everyone; why not try to use most of it when the situation requires it? You know you're beat, but you can't fold. Too much in the pot, too many outs, blinds are about to increase, etc. Whatever the case may be, you will need luck to win. Everyone else is getting lucky against you, now it's time to get lucky against them.

14. Section 14 talks about making new moves. If you don't make new moves, your opponents will eventually read you like a book. By making new moves (even if it means risking your tournament bankroll) you'll display an unpredictable image to your opponents. This will keep them guessing and help you win more pots, tournaments and sessions.

15. Section 15 talks about picking the right games; games that not only fit your style, but your bankroll and experience as well. Play games where you are comfortable at. Don't play a game where you don't have any experience at or your bankroll can't handle or afford.

16. Section 16 and 17 are all about playing poker for a living, whether it's live poker or online

poker. If you want to be a professional, you must have all the skills it requires. I think in my first book (and other books you may have read) as well as this one, you're on the right path of pursuing that dream. Make sure you take the proper steps in becoming a professional. Cover all the angles and assure yourself you are ready.

17. Section 18 and 19 are all about acting on your reads and listening to your instincts. This section is very important when playing poker. Your reads and instincts will more often than most tell you what play you need to make. If your instincts are strong enough, you'll make the correct play almost every time. Fold when you sense you are beat and call, raise or re-raise when you sense weakness.

18. Section 20 covers: small pots vs. large pots. All pots are important, but you can't win them all. Focus more on the larger pots, but don't ignore the small pots. Small pots will help you out with the increased blinds in a tournament as well as a little extra cash in your pocket during a cash game.

19. Section 21 talks about how having fun will equal more wins. If you and the players around you are relaxed and having fun, winning money will be easier. A friendly home game is easier to win than casino table filled

with upset and mad regulars who are their, not to make friends, but to win your money at any cost, even making odd call where they get extremely lucky against you.

20. Section 22 is all about how to talk less at the tables. Talking less at the tables will provide you with less of "your" valuable information to leak out. Keep all poker information to yourself, so that no one gains from it. But keep it friendly with non-poker related conversations. Or, if it does involved poker, then make sure it's clean, wholesome fun, not involving negative things.

21. Section 23 is all about advance position. Position is important in any poker game. Learn as much as you can about position and I guarantee you it will help you in pursuit of being successful.

22. Section 24 covers: doing the obvious. When the pot is larger than normal or you want to protect your hand, then playing obvious to your opponents is the best play. Most hands you'll mix it, but certain hands need to be played obviously to assure the win.

23. Section 25 is about mix it up. You always need to mix it up against the right opponents. Occasionally you'll play a hand more obvious, but the majority of the time you'll need to learn when to play a hand differently against

different opponents. You'll also need to learn when to play a hand you wouldn't normally to keep your opponents guessing.

24. Section 26 is all about taking your time at the tables. By taking your time, you'll be able to put the story of your opponents hand easier and more accurately. Taking your time in every situation will also help you conceal the strength or weakness of your own hand.

25. Section 27 is about playing rags like the nuts. We all know how to play the nuts for full value, but occasionally you'll need to learn how to play rags like nuts. To keep your opponents guessing, you'll need to learn how to win pots with extremely weak hands, when played for strength.

26. Section 28 covers: knowing when you're beat. You obviously have to know when you have the best hand as well as knowing when you're beat. To separate the difference, simply watch and study your opponents. See how they play every hand in every situation/ position. If you sense you are beat and can't force your opponent to fold, then folding is your only play.

27. Section 29 and 30 are all about moving up into bigger game and moving down into smaller games. Experience and bankroll will justify when to make either move. Move up

when everything is going right. Move down when everything is going wrong.

28. Section 31 is all about traveling. Understanding and adjusting your spending around traveling, all while winning enough at the tables. You always have to put a little aside for travel expenses before making the move to games that are not locally.

29. Section 32 covers: televisions exposure. Being able to handle all the hype and media that surrounds poker. A lot of new players are unable to adjust to it and make blundering plays at the poker table, which could cost them thousands of dollars. Ignore the fame, hype and television spotlight and focus only on the cards and the players around you.

30. Section 33 and 34 talk about fame and fortune and the support from your family and friends. Fame and fortune is what everyone in poker wants, but you must learn how to obtain, manage it and earn more from it. You also have to earn the support from you family and friends. Support is a great pick me up when playing poker. Keeping everyone informed of your status without the risk of losing it all (your bankroll), or more, will make the transition of support go a lot smoother.

31. Section 35 is all about mental poker and its stress. You must have a high level of

Ryan Sleeper

understanding on mental poker as well as understanding and dealing with the stress behind it. Success is hard enough, but with the right mental abilities and capability to handle the stress; your path to victory will be a little easier and more productive quicker.

32. Section 36 covers: playing too many hands. A lot of players play too many hands that result their status for early exits and empty pockets. Learn to fold hands that might look good under aggressive pots/opponents and don't be afraid to fold a big hand to an opponent you feel may have a bigger hand. Folding will save your bankroll, where as calling can leave you broke. Call, raise and re-raise when the time is right. Fold when you know you're beat.

33. Section 37 talks about if an opponent really has the hand he is trying to represent. Simply put the story together on the type of player he is and narrow down the possible hands he could be holding. He may be trying to represent a flush, but is actually sitting there with middle pair.

34. Section 38 is all about reading other poker books. Poker books are great forms of information and also, great forms of entertainment. To be successful you must gather as much information as you can about

every opponent. Why not make it a little easier on yourself and be a little more prepared at the table by reading information that's right at your finger tips – a poker book.

35. Section 39 is all about table image. Image of your opponent can be displayed to help you make better decisions as well as your own image to help disguise and confuse your opponents sitting across from you.

36. Section 40 is putting all the pieces together, which we just finished doing. With basic and intermediate strategies as well as the information in this book, you're on your way to becoming a great success in the poker world.

37. Section 41 is the bonus concept: Raising for a free card. The name itself explains what this section is all about. Being aggressive and raising with mediocre hands or draws to receive a free card on the turn or river, where your opponent will most likely not put you on and pay you off.

BONUS CONCEPT: ♠
RAISING FOR A FREE CARD

Raising for a free card is a great way to make a made hand for a minimum price. When you choose to raise an opponents bet, you'll most likely gain control of the pot, resulting your opponent to slow down and check on the next street. With this in mind, you'll be able to check as well (if you choose to) so you can see a free card on the turn or river that might help your hand, at no cost at all. If your opponent does not back down on the turn, then you know he has a good hand, and a fold might be your best play.

This kind of play is very important to make when playing against the top professionals. All good players are aggressive and want action on every round (unless they sense strength by their opponent and choose to slow down). If you gain control of the pot by raising with a mediocre hand or draw, your opponent may step back and play passively to you. On the turn you can now decide what play is best. Sometimes you'll bet out, other times you'll check to see a free river card. Either or, you'll be able to see a free card for a price less than what your opponent had in mind.

The best time to raise is on the flop. No matter what happened pre-flop, you're choosing to raise on the flop because you feel your opponent may be weak or have no greater than top pair. With your raise, you feel he/she will not re-raise you and either fold or just flat call. On the next street you're able to make the correct play depending on your opponent and what you feel he/she is holding. If you decide to check, then let's hope you hit your much-needed card on the river, because most likely your opponent will bet out thinking you are weak. If you bet out, then chances are your opponent may check and call or check and fold. Either or, his aggressiveness pre-flop is now overpowered by your aggressiveness post-flop. No matter what hits the river, you must bet if you choose to bet on the turn. You may be surprised if your opponent ends up folding top pair, thinking his hand was no good.

Making this type of play may not work against everyone; only a select few: tight players and tight-aggressive players. On the rare occasion a looser player may fold, if he feels he is beat. I wouldn't be surprised if he calls you down. If he feels you are capable of making crazy raises with mediocre hands or considers you a loose player as well, then he just may call your bets. Making this play against a calling station is not a good move either. Since these types of players will almost call anything, you're less likely to pull the bluff if he is sitting there with middle pair or better. Of course, if you hit your hand, then you'll most likely get paid off.

With this concept, you can't always just check and call. Occasionally you must raise to gain control of the pot and the pot size. With draws and mediocre hands, sometimes, you'll have to raise (when you sense weakness) to see a free card on the turn or river. By doing so, your opponents will not always read you as holding strength every time you raise. By raising with draws, middle or bottom pair, you'll have your opponents constantly guessing what you're holding. Since they can't read you, you'll be able to take down more pots without having a made hand.

ARE YOU A ROOKIE, AMATEUR OR PRO?

This section will cover the basic questions of determining whether or not you're a rookie, amateur or a professional. Of course, these are not the only questions that will cover your status, but it will focus more on the important questions to see whether or not your level, right now, is that of a professional.

1. Is poker your only source of income?

2. Do you travel to play poker in other states or countries?

3. Do you only play in home games?

4. Do you mostly play in homes games, while sometimes play in casinos?

5. Do you only play on the internet?

6. Do you play for free or for money on the internet?

7. What stakes do you play? Are they of a status where professionals would play?

_____

8. How many years experience do you have?

_____

9. Are you a winner?

_____

10. Do you break even?

_____

11. Do you always lose?

_____

12. Do you have a side bankroll just for poker?

_____

13. Do you play cash games on a regular basis?

_____

14. Do you play tournaments on a regular basis?

_____

15. Are you gradually moving up into bigger games?

_____

16. Do you pay taxes through your poker winnings, as stated as a job?

_____

17. Have you ever been on television playing poker?

_____

18. Do you have any major wins under your belt where the prize pool was over $50,000?

_____

19. Do you have any major wins under your belt where the prize pool has been over $100,000?

_____

20. Do you have any major wins under your belt where the prize pool has been over $500,000?

_____

21. Do you have any major wins under your belt where the prize pool has been over $100,000,000?

_____

22. Are you a WSOP, WPT, Aussie Millions or any other event winner of this status?

_____

23. Do you keep track of your record wins and loses at different places as well as different types of games?

_____

24. Are you known around the poker world? Saying, if you walked into the WSOP, players and non-players would greet you and/or ask for an autograph?

_____

25. Are you a rookie, amateur or a professional?

_____

_____

_____

_____

_____

_____

If you answered, "yes" to most of these questions, then you're most likely a professional. Obviously the questions about money, wins and productive status are more directed towards players who are labeled as a "professional."

If you fall short and answer a lot of, "no" or fail to answer the more important questions, which were previously stated in the professional section with a "yes", then you're probably an amateur (maybe still a rookie). You're reaching the status of a professional, but something is holding you back. Keep working on your game and find the missing links on what it takes to be a professional.

If you answered more "no" than "yes", then you are most likely a rookie. No need to be ashamed, just continue to do your work and find ways to improve your game. One day you'll be a professional.

RANKINGS OF YOUR POKER LEVEL ♦

To determine the level of your poker status, referring to your skills on the table in comparison to the title of your level; rookie, amateur or pro, you must analyze your capabilities of actions that take place on the felt. Similar to the previous section, but here we will talk about your actions on the table in comparison to what level you're playing at or the level you should be playing at if you want to be a professional.

Here are some questions and answers that will help you determine your level of a poker player. At the end, put together your theory on your level ranking to that of a poker player; rookie, amateur or a professional. Do you think you might be a professional, simply by the actions you make at the poker table?

Answer 1 will be referring to the rookies or amateurs and Answer 2 will refer to the professionals.

1. *Can you fold top pair, while in middle position, when a tight player bets pot on the flop, from first position?*

Answer 1:

Most rookies and amateurs can not fold their top pair, simply because they see there hand being a level of strength, not realizing that the tight player betting in first position is holding, most likely, 2 pair or better. They will most likely call this opponent down to the river and unless he improves, he'll lose a large pot to a player who played his hand obvious to the title of his image.

Answer 2:

A professional sees that the person betting in first position is tight and would only make that large of a bet, in that position, with no less than 2 pair. He is capable of folding his top pair, especially if his kicker is weak or he has no backdoor draws.

2. *Can you raise pre-flop with a weak hand and continue to be aggressive with it all the way to the river, no matter what hits the flop, especially when you sense weakness from your opponent?*

Answer 1:

Rookie or amateurs are not able to pull off this kind of bluff successfully. They may try it from to time, but usually back off when their opponent is playing right along with them. They will most likely give up the pot or call an opponent's bet and lose when they don't improve. If they do try to pull the trigger on every round against an opponent who is calling him down, then he'll most likely lose the pot to a better hand.

Answer 2:

A professional has the courage to make aggressive bets and raises on every street in his continued streak to steal the pot. If he feels his opponent has a hand that will not be forced to fold, he may slow his actions down. He showed aggressions pre-flop and will most likely continue it to the river, unless otherwise stated.

3. *Can you raise an opponents bet on the flop or turn when you know he has a good hand, but feel he may fold?*

Answer 1:

A rookie or amateur will raise when they have a big hand. Very rarely will this caliber of player raise an opponents bet when he knows he is beat. To be successful you must be able to force an opponent to fold when you know he has you beat. If you can make him think you have a stronger hand, then a raise could be the correct play.

Answer 2:

A professional can easily make this play against the proper opponent. He knows his game well enough to make such a daring raise. His read on his opponent vs. the read he feels his opponent has on him and concluded to the answer to raise. He feels his opponent will fold to a raise, sensing his opponent may only have top or middle pair.

4. *Can you fold a monster starting hand pre-flop, like A-K, A-Q, Pocket Queens, Jacks or 10's (possibly pocket kings as well)?*

Answer 1:

A rookie or amateur will almost never fold one of these starting hands pre-flop. They see a strong starting and will play it for any amount. They don't realize that their opponent could be sitting there with a stronger hand based on his position and how he played his hand.

Answer 2:

A professional has no problem folding any hand (besides aces) pre-flop against an opponent he senses has a strong hand. A professional can read better (than other players) if he is beat, based on his opponent's actions. If he feels his pocket pair or A-k is beat (even pre-flop) he will simply fold the hand and think nothing of it.

5. *Can you raise or re-raise, on any street, with any hand less valuable then what's possible on the board?*

Answer 1:

A rookie or amateur, like I've mentioned before will make most his raises with strong hands. Rarely will he raise with weakness; with middle pair or a draw. Once and a while he may raise with a weak hand, but I wouldn't stress over it too much.

Answer 2:

A professional will raise with any hand at any time when he feels his opponent is weak. Occasionally he will call to extract an extra bet on the next street, but most of the time he will raise any time he senses weakness from any of his opponents.

6. *Can you leave the table when you're running bad and losing?*

Answer 1:

When a rookie or amateur starts losing at the poker table, he'll most likely keep playing there until he wins or breaks even. Most of the time that person will go broke. They don't sense that the table they are at is not a good one and what they should be doing is leaving the table to find a new one or stop playing for the day.

Answer 2:

A professional will leave any game if he feels the table is running bad or he knows he can't beat the game and win his money back. He will either break for the day or a find a table he knows he can beat. He may even move down a level in attempts to earn his lost money back.

7. *How often do you play your hand vs. playing just your opponents hand?*

Answer 1:

A rookie or amateur will play his hand (and only his hand) the majority of the time. I wouldn't look any lower than 80% of the time. From time to time they may play their opponents have over theirs, but that only happens when their opponent is playing a hand so obvious, anyone can read them.

Answer 2:

A professional will play both hands almost equally; about 50% his hand and about 50% his opponents hand. It all depends on his opponents and the situation at hand. Pre-flop, a professional will play his hand a high majority of the time, but will play his position and his opponents hand quite often, overlooking his own hand. Post-flop he will play his opponents hands more than his own hand. Once he has a read on his opponent's hand, he can ignore what he is holding and just playing his opponents.

8. *Can you be successful in both cash games and tournaments with the same set of strategies?*

Answer 1:

A rookie or amateur usually fails to realize that it takes two sets of strategies to win in both games. If you play the same style in both games, you will lose. You may do well in one game, but will definitely lose in the other game. Focus on the style you have that fits best in either game and play that particular game more often.

Answer 2:

A professional will focus more on one game than the other, simply because he knows his level of skills at that particular game. Occasionally he may play the other game, but will play it with caution until he has a good grasp on how the game and his opponents play out. There are really only about a dozen of professionals that can be successful in both cash games and tournaments. They have extensive experience and understandings in both games to pull off that rare ability.

9. *Can you oblige from what your instincts (or reads) tell you?*

Answer 1:

A rookie or amateur will rarely act on their instincts or reads. They mostly just play their cards and the bets being made. I feel that their instincts are still in learning process and are unable to make accurate decisions based on them. Over time, with hard work, their instincts and reads will get stronger and at that point they should be considering making plays based solely on that.

Answer 2:

A professional is a professional by making great reads, so they are already at a point in their career where a lot of decisions are made based just on their instincts. They've done their homework and their reads are quite accurate. A lot of decisions will be unclear to the naked eye, but your instincts will help you decide what play is best – when your status is of at a professional.

10. *Are you capable of folding a big hand on the turn or river? A hand like: 2 pair, trips, a straight or a flush. Could you even imagine folding a hand even stronger, like a full house?*

Answer 1:

Very rarely will a rookie or amateur fold a big hand. They see strength and will call almost any bet or raise. If they feel they may be beat, they will simply check-call all the way to the river. Since their game is still in the learning process, they are unable to see the signs when their opponent is showing strength.

Answer 2:

A professional has no problem folding any hand at any time when they sense they are beat. It's hard to fold big hands, but when your instincts and your reads on your opponents are strong − with them showing strength by the way they played their hand, then it's easy to make the fold. Most professionals will check-call in hopes of their hand being best, but when the situation calls for it, he will fold his second best hand.

11. *Can you analyze all the angles before making the correct move? Do you understand what angles need to be noticed as well as making the proper adjustments from them?*

Answer1:

A rookie or amateur will look at the obvious things when making their play. But what they wont' do is assure themselves that all the angles are covered. They may look at just hand value or pot odds, failing to see player knowledge, player tells, position of his opponent and the hand he could be holding by the way he played it, chip stacks and making the proper play just by that alone and etc.

Answer 2:

A professional will look at all angles before making his move. He will put the entire story together so that when he decides to fold, call or raise he is assuring himself he is making the right play. He will first look at his opponent's position pre-flop and categorize what hands he likes to play from that position. Of course, his chip stack will also determine is holdings. Short stacked, he may be holding a mediocre hand, because he would have most likely pushed all in with a big hand. Large stack, he could be holding any hand, depending on the type of player he is and the position he is holding pre-flop and post-flop. Second, he will look at how he played his hand post-flop. By this time he should have a pretty good read on what his opponent is holding. Chip stacks at this point are also important as well as "tells" and other information you should have gathered by now. Lastly, the professional will make the correct play when the story adds up. If he is beat and can't force his opponent to fold, then he will muck his hand, otherwise he will call or raise based on the read he has on him.

Here is just one example of a player who didn't look at all the angles before making his play. It was in a live tournament, near the middle stages of it, and I was getting short stacked. I am in middle position and decided to push all in with A♥-3♥. Everyone folded to the player in the big blind. He looked at his cards, then look at the price is was going to cost him. He realized that it would only cost him another big blind to make the call. No matter what he was holding he should make the call, right? Wrong. What he didn't realize is that, yes, it was only costing him another big blind to make the call and possibly knock an opponent out, but what he didn't realize was the fact that if he called, and lost, he would only have a few chips less; an amount far less than even the price of a small blind. Well, he decided to call and lost the pot when an Ace hit the flop. He was holding 9♦-5♣. True, it was only costing him a small amount, but it was amount he didn't realize that in actuality cost him his entire tournament. He didn't have enough chips to make a move later in the round, so he made his early exit a couple hands later.

12. *Are you capable of laying a hand down to a check-raise, especially one coming from a player who only normally raises with big hands?*

Answer 1:

If a rookie or amateur bets out on the flop, normally in late position after a few players have checked, and someone decides to check-raise, they will normally call the bet with any pair or any draw. They don't realize that this check-raise most likely means a monster hand; usually 2 pair or better. But of course, they see some strength in their hand or they love draws to the river, so they decide to call. More often than most they will fold on the turn or just flat out lose the pot on the river when they fail to improve their hand. Your opponent is most likely check-raising to extract a bet from a player in later position. Sometimes a check-raise will be a big draw, but more often than most, when a player check-raises, it means he has a strong hand, and unless you have a big hand yourself, you should be folding.

Answer 2:

A professional has no problem folding to a check-raise if he feels his opponent would only make that play with strength. If he feels his opponent is capable of check-raising with a weaker hand, than he will either call or re-raise him back. It all depends on the player and each of their positions and the action that took place pre-flop. A professional is known to check-raise with weaker hands if he feels the bettor is weak, himself. A professional is extremely talented at mixing up his play, so playing against them for a check-raise could be a confusing move defensively.

13. *Do you always defend your blind or are you capable of letting a blind go for even a small cost?*

Answer 1:

A rookie or amateur will almost always defend their blind, even at double the blind price (more often the rookie than the amateur). They fail to see the position the raiser and the style he plays as well as the fact that he is out of position throughout the entire hand (acting first on every round). We all want to act last during a hand, but too many players defend their blinds out of position, when acting first post-flop, and end up losing more than they bargained for. Don't look at the price of the raise, but look at the player, the player knowledge and the position of each player.

Answer 2:

A professional will give up his blind at any price if he feels his opponent doing the raising is a tight player who only raises with big hands. A professional sees that he will be out of position the entire hand and will fold any weak ace, any weak face card as well as any hand that might seem somewhat valuable. In some cases he may call the raise if the pot is multi-way and he has a hand with great implied odds: suited connectors, unsuited connectors, medium face cards and he knows he can outplay his opponent(s).

14. *Can your opponents chip stack alter your decision-making?*

Answer 1:

A rookie or amateur very rarely scopes out their opponents chip stacks before making a play. Since they mostly play their hand and sometimes position, they often miss the stacks that sit in front of their opponents. Quite often they will limp in or raise from an early or middle position with a weak hand, not realizing that the player in the small or big blind are about to go all in. If they would have checked out the chip stacks before making their play, they could have saved a few (or sometimes a lot) of chips.

Answer 2:

A professional always knows the chip stacks, he and everyone else at the table has in front of them. Before he makes any play, he will process who's in the blind, who is short stacked, who is tight, who is loose, who is giving off a "tell" and etc. A professional will analyze everything, even chip stacks, before deciding to play a hand.

CONCLUSION

In conclusion, we have just covered a lot of advanced concepts for all No Limit Hold'em games. Understanding them and using them correctly will help you become a better poker player. I can guarantee it. So many players today fail to understand these concepts and unconsciously rely solely on luck. They may feel like they are playing correctly, but they don't realize how wrong they are actually playing. They could be sitting down at the table, making great calls on the flop, turn or river and end up winning a lot of money. But what they don't realize is that the luck or the off-balanced of their opponents play was just performed "that" day. This level of success is capable for any player, but not the type of success that can make you a professional. Play against these same opponents day-in-and-day-out and see how it changes. Your plays may not work the next time nor will the luck be there...helping you out. I wouldn't be surprised if ultimately you went broke.

Most people today think that their style of play is the correct one; focusing on luck and "what they call" their strong instincts, reads or "feel". They also think their abnormal plays are correct in those spots. They may make odd calls, raises or check-raises and end up winning the pot, not realizing that, that play worked that time, but I'm almost certain it won't work again. You may have caught a good run of cards or luck or even against an opponent who wouldn't normally fold in that spot, where he was actually holding the best hand. If your opponents are more skilled, then I can assure you, they won't make that mistake again. They will simply adjust their game to yours, so that they make the correct play in their next involvement.

By understanding these advanced concepts, and they are advanced to the average player that plays today, you'll understand more on making the correct play based on different variables. You'll be able to cover all the angles of the play and comply with the best decision. Learning and using these concepts correctly will declare your increasing bankroll status as well as your poker status – as a professional. All professionals today (well, a majority of them) understand all these concepts and uses them correctly more often than not. These new professionals that have only won 1 major tournament or is a success on the internet may not know all these concepts. They may be a short-term success, in the process of learning these concepts, but as of today they are not capable of being a true professional. I think they will in time, but right now you have the edge, because you're reading this book. Whether you're successful right now or not, by reading these concepts, you'll have a mental edge against the average player, even if he does have more money and more tournaments wins than you. With consistency and increased knowledge, you'll overpass his level and become a greater, more successful player. And all you did was buy a book.

GLOSSARY ♥

Some of these words you may not find mentioned in this book, but it's important to know them. A few of them are just alternate sayings with the same definition.

Advertising:

To display one image or style of play to switch it up in future hands. Showing a bluff early on to assure value for a later hand on. Or playing tight and only showing big hands to pull off a bluff later in the game.

All-In:

Having all of one's money in the pot. To bet everything you have in front of you.

Back Door:

The term is used for a hand made on 4th and 5th street that a player wasn't originally trying to make. It also means to catching runner-runner.

Bad Beat:

Having a hand that was a big favorite to win, only to be defeated as a result of a lucky draw.

Bankroll:

The amount of money you have available to wager.

Belly Buster:

A draw to an inside straight; also called a "gut shot." If the flop is 2♦-3♠-5♣ and you hold an Ace and a 6, only the 4 will give you the straight, so you're on a belly buster or gut-shot draw.

Bet:

To put money in the pot before anyone else has. This action is made post-flop.

Bettor:

The first person to put money in the pot, on any given round.

Bet for Value:

To bet a small amount in order to be called by a lesser valued hand. You are betting to make money, not to make your opponents fold, because you know you have the best hand.

Blank:

A card that is not of any value to a player's hand.

Blinds:

A forced bet that one or more players must make to start the action on the first round of betting. The blind rotates around the table with each new deal.

Bluff:

A bet or raise with a hand you do not think is the best hand. Normally betting or raising with no pair or draw.

Board:
The community cards in the center of the table.

Bottom Pair:
Pairing the lowest card on the board.

Button:
The Dealer.

Buy-In:
The minimum amount of money required to sit down in a particular game.

Call:
To put in the pot the amount of money equal to an opponent's bet or raise.

Call a Raise Cold:
To call a double bet (a bet and a raise).

Caller:
A person who calls the bet or raise.

Chase:
To continue a hand trying to outdraw an opponent's hand you are quite sure is better than yours. A lot of players like to chase for an over card. If the flop is 3♦-6♣-9♠ and your opponent is holding A♥-Q♠ he might call you "chasing" for an over card (Ace or Queen).

Check:

To decline to bet when it is your turn, passing the action to the player next to act.

Check-Raise:

To check and then raise after an opponent bets.

Cold Deck:

A situation where it seemed like the deck was stacked. Multiple players with big hands that are rarely seen at the same time. For example, one player has pocket Aces against 2 opponents with pocket Kings or Queens. Also, called a "cooler."

Community Cards:

The cards dealt face up in the center of the table that is shared by all the active players.

Continuation Bet:

Making a bet post-flop after you have raised pre-flop, no matter if you hit the flop or not.

Dead Hand:

A hand a player may not continue to play because of an irregularity. Usually when a player violates a rule. Examples: (1) showing a hand to an opponent before all action is completed. (2) Turning your cards face up before an opponent calls or before a turn or river card is exposed.

Dead Money:

Money put in the pot by players who have already folded their hands.

Drawing Dead:

Drawing to try to make a hand that cannot possibly win, because an opponent already holds a bigger (made) hand or the nuts.

Draw Out:

To improve your hand so that it beats an opponent who had a better hand than yours, prior to your draw or hand of lesser value.

Double Belly Buster:

Four cards to a straight, which can be made with cards of two different ranks. If the board is 7♠-9♥-10♦-K♣ and you hold Q♦-8♠, then a 6 or Jack will give you the straight. Giving you 8 outs instead of 4 outs like a gut-shot would.

Early Position:

A position on a round of betting in which you must act before most of the other players.

Edge:

An advantage over an opponent.

Expectation:

The average profit or loss of any bet over the long run.

Favorite:

A hand that has the best chance of winning.

Family Pot:
A pot: in which most or all the players at the table are involved.

Fifth Street:
The fifth and final community card on the board. Also called "The River."

Flat Call:
To call a bet without raising.

Flop:
The first 3 exposed community cards, which are dealt simultaneously.

Flush:
Five cards of the same suit.

Fold:
To drop out of a hand rather than calling a bet or raise. To "muck"

Four-Flush:
Four cards to a flush.

Four of a Kind:
Four cards of the same rank. Also called "quads".

Fourth Street:
The fourth community card on the board. Also called "The Turn."

Free Card:

A card that a player gets without having to call a bet.

Free Rolling:

A situation where two players have the same hand, but one of them has a chance to make a better hand. Ace King off suit vs. Ace King suited, meaning they have the same hand but the suited Ace King has a chance of winning with a flush. The player with the suited cards is "free rolling"; especially when the board has given the suited cards a flush draw.

Full House:

Having three cards of one rank and two cards of another rank. Three of a kind and a pair: 3 three's and 2 two's in one hand.

Giving a Hand Away:

Playing your hand in such a way that your opponents should know what you have.

Good Game:

A game, in which there are enough players worse than you, for you to be a substantial favorite.

Gut Shot:

When you're drawing to an inside straight. Also called "a belly buster." You're holding 8♣-9♥ and the board is A♠-5♦-6♥, meaning you need the 7 (4 outs) to catch your straight. A card, in the middle of the draw, that will complete it.

Heads-Up:

Playing against only one other player.

Hourly Rate:

The amount of money a player expects to win per hour on average.

Implied Odds:

The ratio of the total amount of money you expect to win if you make your hand to the bet you must now call to continue in the hand.

Kicker:

A side card. If the board is 2♦-4♠-6♣-7♥-10♥ and you hold A♣-10♠ while your opponent holds King-10, then you win because you have a higher kicker with your Ace to his King.

Late Position:

Positions on a round of betting, in which you act after most of the other players have acted.

Limit:

The amount a player may bet or raise on any round of betting.

Limp In:

To call a bet rather than raise. (Pre-flop Action)

Live Cards:

Having 2 cards not matching your opponent(s) cards. All in pre-flop and you have Q♥-J♣. Your opponent has A♦-K♠. You have live cards because none of your cards match any of your opponent(s) cards.

Live One:

A loose, weak player with a lot of money to lose.

Lock (also look up "nuts" or "pure nuts"):

A cinch hand. A hand that cannot lose.

Long Shot:

A hand that has little chance of being made. Calling bets and raises with a slim number of outs.

Loose:

Playing more hands that normal.

Loose Game:

A game with a lot of players in most pots.

Middle Pair:

Pairing the second highest card on the board.

Middle Position:

A position, on a round of betting, somewhere in the middle.

Muck:

To discard you hand. To "fold".

Multi-way Pot:

A pot in which two or more players are involved.

Nuts:

The best possible hand at any given point in the pot. If you flop the nut straight, meaning the flop is 10♦-J♣-Q♠ and you're holding A♥-K♣. You have the best possible hand (or nuts) on the flop.

Odds:

The ratio of the amount of money in the pot to the bet you must call to continue with the hand.

Off-Suit:

Two cards: Not of the same suit.

On Tilt:

Playing much worse than usual, because you've come emotionally upset. Usually happens when you have a bad beat. Also called "steaming."

Open-Ended Straight:

Four consecutive cards to a straight, which can be made with, two cards of different ranks. If you fold 9♠-10♣ and the flop is 2♥-8♦-J♠ then you have 8 outs to give you the straight. A 7 or Queen will complete it. The ends of a straight.

Outs:

Cards left in the deck, which will improve your hand.

Overcall:

A call or bet after another player has already called.

Over-card:
A card higher than any other card on the flop or any card higher than those in your hand.

Over-pair:
A wired pair that is higher that any card on the board.

Pair:
Two cards of the same rank.

Pass:
To check or fold.

Pay-Off:
To call a bet or raise when you don't think you have the best hand.

Position:
The spot in the sequence of betting in which a player is located.

Pot:
The total amount of money wagered at any point in the hand.

Pot Committed:
Forced to call a bet when most of your money is in the pot. I don't believe in pot committed; because I feel you can fold at any time, even when know you're beat, no matter how much is in the pot.

Pot Odds:

The ratio of the amount of money in the pot to the bet you must call to continue with the hand. When your opponent bets $50 into a $200 pot, then you're getting 4 to 1 on your money. 200 divided by 50 = 4.

Pre-flop:

The action that is taken place before the flop. The action once everyone has his or her 2 down cards.

Put Someone on a Hand:

To determine as best as you can the hand(s) an opponent is most likely holding.

Pure Nuts:

The BEST possible hand. Usually referred to after the river card is dealt.

Rag:

A card that doesn't complete any possible draws. Also called a "blank".

Raise:

To bet an additional amount after someone else has bet. A raise must be at least double the original bet.

Raiser:

A player who raises.

Rake:

An amount retained by the casino (or house) from each pot. Rakes are normally taken from cash games only, not tournaments. Tournaments have fees, which are taken from the original buy-in.

Represent:

To make your opponents believe you have a better hand than you really do. This is also a form of bluffing.

Re-Raise:

To raise after an opponent has raised.

Reverse Implied Odds:

The ratio of the amount of money now in the pot to the amount of money you will have to call to continue from the present round to the end of the hand.

Round of Betting:

A sequence of betting after one or more cards has been dealt.

Royal Flush:

An ace-high straight flush. The best possible hand in poker.

Running Pair:

Fourth and Fifth Street cards of the same rank. For example, you hold A♥- 7♣ and the board is 8♠-9♦-Q♥. To catch a running pair you'll need both the turn and river to be either 7's or both Aces'.

Rush:

Several winnings in a short period of time.

Second Pair:

Pairing the second highest card on the board.

Semi-Bluff:

To bet with a hand, which you do not think, is the best hand, but which has a reasonable chance of improving to the best hand.

Set:

Three of a kind, when you hold a pocket pair and a third one hits the board. For example, you're holding pocket 6's and the flop is 2♣-6♠-10♥.

Short-Stacked:

Playing in a game with a relatively fewer number of chips remaining. Having fewer chips than most players at your table.

Showdown:

The turning up of all active players' cards at the end of the final round of betting, to see who has the best hand.

Side Pot:

A second pot for the other active players when one player is all in.

Slow-Play:

To check or just call an opponent's bet with a big hand in order to in more money on later rounds of betting.

Slow Rolling:

To delay an easy call. You know you have the best hand, but you take longer that you should to make the call or show your hand.

Small Ball:

A strategy of seeing flops cheaply to either win a big pot by connecting with rags or a small pot by outplaying weaker opponents without risking too much.

Starting Requirements:

The minimum initial hand, a player considers he needs to continue in the pot.

Start the Action:

To make the first bet in a particular hand.

Steal:

To cause your opponents to fold when you probably do not have the best hand. Could also be labeled as a bluff.

Straight:

Five cards of mixed suits in sequence.

Straight Flush:

Five cards of the same suit in sequence.

Structure:

The limits set upon the ante, forced bets and subsequent bets and raises in any given game.

Sucker:

A player who can be expected to lose money. An inexperienced player.

Suited:

Two or more cards of the same suit.

Tell:

A mannerism a player exhibits that may give away the strength or weakness of his hand.

Three of a Kind:

Three cards of the same rank. Also called "Trips"

Tight:

Playing fewer hands than the norm. Playing only premium hands and playing just your cards and not your opponents.

Tight Game:

A game with a small number of players in most pots.

Tilt:

When you don't play your normal style after taking a bad beat. You let your emotions take over the game, making too many bad decisions.

Top Pair:

Pairing the highest card on the board.

Trips:
Three of a kind.

Turn:
The fourth community card. Also called "The Turn."

Two-Flush:
Two cards of the same suit.

Underdog:
A hand that does not have the best chance of winning.

Under the Gun:
The first person to act on the first round of betting. (Pre-flop action)

Value:
What a hand is worth in terms of its chance of being the best hand.

Value Bet:
Making a small bet into a large pot to gain an extra bet.

Walk:
To be in the big blind (pre-flop) and everyone folds to you. Winning the pot uncontested.

Wired Pair:
A pair in the hole. Also called a "pocket pair."